PRECIOUS GEMS

A BLAKE BROTHERS NOVEL

SIERRA HILL

❀ Created with Vellum

PREFACE

He is my darkness. An obsidian knight – powerful, protective and strong.

He brought me comfort in a time of pain. Peace in a time of loss. Sustenance when I was hungry. His strength shielded me from the harsh, piercing lights of the world.

Like precious gems carved in the dark recesses of the earth, shaped by the great pressure and intense heat of the earth, I too was shaped by him.

Just as minerals are forced together through a tumultuous process to metamorphose and change into something different, I was changed into something beautiful.

Something fragile yet strong.

Something crystallized and made to withstand all other external forces that push against it.

His dark shaped me. Made me new.

He is my dark.

And I am his precious gem.

PROLOGUE

B*efore*

THE SMACK across my face is sudden and jarring.

My head snaps up, jaw widening to allow the escape of a soft gasp, my open palm covering my cheek where the skin burns hot from his hand.

"Don't you fuck this up for me, Gemma. Do you hear me?"

I stare blankly into his eyes, the eyes of a man who I both love and detest, his bloodshot orbs glaring me down with undeniable hatred and disgust.

"Just do exactly what I've told you and do not deviate from the plan. Text me only when you land and once you have the money."

His cold eyes sweep over my body, his lips quivering with hostility, his breath reeking of alcohol and cigarettes.

My father hates me for reasons I may never fully understand. And yet, I continue to try, time and time again, to gain his love and approval.

"And keep that fucking mouth and whoring legs of yours shut. You know what will happen if I find out you've done something stupid, don't you?"

It's not a question. Whether I'm too quiet, or too loud, or I sneeze, or am two minutes late – there are always consequences. And his words hurt me more and cause more damage than any slap or punch could ever do.

I simply nod my head and stare up into the eyes of the only parent I have ever known as he lifts the heavy backpack and straps it over my shoulder to carry. I accept it with shaking hands, like the gauntlet given to a warrior who heads off to war.

I'm the chosen warrior this time but still the lowly servant to his majesty.

It isn't that he trusts me anymore than he did yesterday, or that he believes I'm ready to step up into a new role in this family. No, the only reason I've been tasked with this assignment now is that there's no one else around he can trust. Although I wonder if he ever really trusts anyone at all.

Regardless of his intentions, I'm the only one in the family available for this job. The only one in his crew able to leave the country with a passport that won't flag the police or the Feds.

He chose me to go because my name won't appear on any watch list or database because I've never been in trouble with the law. I've kept my nose clean and kept off the radar of the authorities.

I may be the daughter of Mudd Phillips, a known criminal and thief, but this is the first time he's ever involved me in the family business.

And hopefully the only time.

Because after this, I'm gone.

I have plans for the rest of my life.

And they don't involve being a career criminal in my father's connected world.

CHAPTER 1

The woman in the line in front of me lets out a loud grumbling breath, heaving an exaggerated sigh before twisting around to speak to me. She passes a look that indicates we're in cahoots. Which we are not.

"God, does everyone in Europe have to move this slow?"

I keep my head down, eyes averted and stare at the passport in my hand before raising my chin to respond to her question.

"I'm not sure. This is my first time here." I shrug with a shy lift of my shoulder and hope she leaves it at that.

I was given explicit instructions not to talk with anyone. Mudd made that very clear. He wanted me to keep a low profile, to get in and get out, and not raise awareness as to why a girl from Jersey is in Belgium.

But no such luck. The woman pushes her elegantly styled blonde hair out of her face, producing a knowing smile before dropping a well-manicured hand down on my arm. Her gold dangly bracelets jingle loudly, and I flinch at her touch.

I'm not used to the soft and sensitive touch of a woman because I've never had it. I never knew my mother. I have no frame of reference for what the gentle compassion of a fellow woman feels like.

While the foreign feeling catches me off-guard, it is neither wanted nor appreciated.

"Oh, darling. You are going to love Antwerp," she exclaims, a dreamy look sketching across her face. Her eyes dance across my face and body, and she hums. "And with your youth and beauty, you're sure to have swarms of young men flocking around you. Are you staying here in Belgium? Or will you be traveling around Europe?"

An automatic yes is about to leave my lips when I stop myself, remembering my dad's emphatic command. *Keep your fucking mouth shut.*

I mumble a noncommittal response. "Mmm-hmm."

"Are you here to study abroad? Oh my God, you'll have so much fun! I did that when I was in college, too. Had the time of my life." She wiggles her full eyebrows at me, tilting sideways at her hips to whisper, as if I'm in on her secret. "I still have fond memories of Marcello from a weekend in Portugal when I was twenty-something."

The woman runs a finger across her pouty bottom lip, her thoughts taking her far away from the custom's line. I look her over surreptitiously, noting the fine lines around her eyes and mouth, conspicuously hidden by Botox and brightener.

If I had to guess, I'd say she was in her late 30's, maybe early 40's. Her outfit is fancy, bling and baubles, expensive handbag and shoes. Definitely a socialite or a woman of wealth and money.

She flutters a hand over her face, as if she's overheating from the memories, and then darts a hand out in front of her looking for me to accept it.

"My name's Dorian, by the way. And yours, darling?"

Oh shit. Do I give her my real name? I hadn't considered the possibility that I'd have to engage in conversation with anyone aside from the taxi driver who would take me to my destination. In fact, I was sure everyone would be speaking a different language, leaving it impossible to converse.

No such luck.

In the second or two that it takes for me to decide on what information I should share with her, her interest diverts to the sound of incoming messages on her phone she clasps in her hand. She holds it up to read, tapping out a response, as we slowly inch forward another few steps in line.

My mind wanders, and I wonder if she's here for business or pleasure. Maybe she's here for a week-long conference. Or maybe she's meeting a man she's having a torrid love affair with, and they are running away together.

I may have lived a sheltered life thus far, never leaving my home of Jersey, except for some trips here and there to New York City, but my imagination can run wild, dreaming up very vivid and crazy notions.

Wondering what I would do if I was free to travel the world to learn about new cultures and people and to move away from the noise and havoc of Jersey. Out from under my father's cruel thumb and my brother's brutal torment.

The backpack suddenly feels like it weighs a thousand pounds, the contents inside worth more to me than just a profit. It holds the key to my future. And the irony is not lost on me that in order to buy my freedom and cut the ties that bind me to my dad and brother, leaving behind a life of crime, I have to sell a stolen diamond. A crime, in and of itself.

I never wanted to be in this business with my dad and brother. And for a long time, Mudd kept me out of it. But there came when I grew old enough that Mudd figured out that a pretty teenage girl would be useful in their trade. So, he trained me and put me to work.

And not in the same way he focused his energies on my older brother, Johno. A man who at the age of twenty-four, is considered the prince of the family. The next in line to the Phillips empire.

But with Johno now incarcerated in a federal penitentiary in upstate New York, and Mudd in fairly poor health and under house arrest, I was promoted from lackey to mule. Lucky me.

The timing of this deal and the factors leaving me the only one who could handle it for Mudd, gave me the leverage I needed to cut my own deal. I made my father promise me that once I returned, I'd be able to leave and walk away from the conning and thieving, the petty crimes I'd been tasked with for years - and he wouldn't stop me.

To GET the hell away from this family and lead my own life.

At twenty, there's so much I want to do. Maybe go to art school to become an artist. Or move to L.A. to act or Bora Bora and make handmade bracelets for beach vacationers. I don't care where I go or what I do, as long as I can create something. But it won't happen without my father's consent.

But how much can you ever really trust the word of a con man?

The only purpose I have ever served in my father's life was to use my innocence, model looks and my skills in pickpocketing to find an easy mark, create a distraction and take them for all I could. I worked those cons in hopes that one day, he would approve of me. That one day he would finally say, *"Gemma, I love you. You're such a good girl and I'm so glad you're my daughter."*

But that's just me romanticizing and dreaming of a fairytale family-life that doesn't exist.

I was raised by a heartless man whose only goal in life is the next con. The next game. He used people and used me for profit.

Love was never something he taught me, demonstrated or bestowed upon me. All the attention he directed toward me was borne of hostility and some deep-rooted hatred, probably manifesting from my mother's betrayal. Maybe, had she not left us when I was a baby, things would've been different. Maybe he loved my mother, and she took all that love with her when she left.

But I'll never know, and it's too late to try and forge a relationship with him. I've tried and only been beaten for it in the past.

The line inches forward, as Dorian receives a phone call. "What?" she answers rudely, a severe contradiction from her sweet tone with me.

Trying to offer her some privacy, I pull out my phone from my purse and text my dad.

Landed safely. Going through customs.

The three dots appear.

Don't fuck up.

I laugh, because honestly, what did I expect?

As we move closer and closer to the customs agent, my nerves begin to knot and fray inside my belly, and I'm suddenly fearful about entering Belgium. Beads of sweat have congregated on my palms, and I wipe the moisture on my pants, swallowing down the dusty lump in my throat, trying desperately to regulate my breathing.

What if the customs agents badger me about my visit? What if they want to check my bag? What if I prove my father right and wind up fucking this all up because my fear wins and I'm an unconvincing liar?

This is exactly what Mudd was worried about when he walked me through this assignment.

"If they ask you, just tell them you're here to see your grand-mother and cousins in Antwerp," he said during the lengthy list of instructions he threw at me the day before I left. "And if they check the bag and ask about the stone, just say it's a family heirloom you're returning to your grandmother."

What seemed plausible at the time now seems like too big of a lie. One that I fear I'll trip over if I'm asked to provide any sort of substantial detail. While I can steal and lie for a con on the streets, I might very well crumble under the direct scrutiny of the uniformed agents, whose sole purpose is to flush out criminals and drug dealers coming into their country.

An idea comes to mind as Dorian ends her call and shakes her head, throwing her phone back into her big leather satchel, hanging on an elbow.

"Excuse me, Dorian. But do you happen to know where I can catch a city bus from here?"

I ask this in the sweetest, Bambi-eyed tone I can muster, trying to appear bewildered and inept, hoping she'll take the bait.

And she does.

She waves a hand in the air to indicate it's the dumbest thing she's heard today. "Oh honey, a young girl like you shouldn't be taking a bus alone. I have a driver waiting at baggage claim, and I can drop you off anywhere in the city you need to go."

Perfect.

Now to turn it on full volume.

"Oh, I'm not sure about that. I mean, I don't know you. You could be one of those sex trafficking madams, luring young women into your business."

She looks genuinely shocked, her eyes widening and hand clutching at her throat. "Oh, dear heavens. That's… that's horrible that we live in a world where strangers can't be kind and helpful. But I promise you, I'm only looking out for you."

And now for the grand finale.

Cause a diversion. A distraction to draw attention away from the con.

My performance is played out flawlessly, as I begin to tear up, the moisture flooding my eyes and down my cheeks as I reach around Dorian to embrace her in a hug.

As I do, I swiftly drop the stone into the side pocket of her satchel, a smile tugging at the corners of my mouth.

"Oh Dorian, I can't believe how wonderful you are. Thank you. I was so scared about being alone and finding my way around the city."

She coos like I'm a cute, helpless baby instead of the twenty-year-old thief that I am.

"Sweetie, it's my pleasure. And girls like you - beautiful and young - you should never be required to take public transportation if it can be helped."

A girl like me?

I'm a Jersey girl who has only ever taken public transportation and could hold her own against the fiercest of thugs.

But she doesn't know the real me. And that's what the con is all about.

CHAPTER 2

My con works like a charm.

Dorian carries the contraband jewel, unbeknownst to her, successfully through customs and waits for me at the baggage claim while I do my best not to stumble over my responses to the questions I'm being asked.

Although the agent's accent throws me for a loop, thankfully the questions he poses were all generic and fairly innocuous, all of which I can respond to honestly. I move through unscathed, if not a little frazzled.

My only problem now is confiscating the jewel back from Dorian's bag and avoiding further interrogation about my purpose here.

Since she seems to think I'm here to study abroad, I decide it's easier to deceive if she already has that objective in her mind. The best deception is using the using a version of the truth and manipulating it into reality.

The task could not be easier as the perfect opportunity presents itself. As we stand at the rotating carousel, Dorian bends over to grab one of her four pieces of Louis Viton luggage, struggling with the weight. She turns to me for assistance.

"Here, darling. Could you hold this for a moment while I grab my bags?"

She hoists the bag into my chest, leaving me to cradle it in my arms like a baby. She then spins around in a flourish and practically topples the old woman next to her as she leans in and grabs the handle of another large designer bag.

My hand pushes down into the smooth leather of the purse, slipping into the side pocket, rooting around for the soft material of the pouch that encases the diamond. Locating it easily, I enclose it in my fist and extract it from the purse, all before Dorian has even lifted her luggage off the conveyor.

I just hope the rest of my trip here is as simple as this.

THE RIDE into the City Center of Antwerp isn't long, but full of interesting stories Dorian shares with me about her college years and her time spent abroad. The woman has certainly lived an interesting, if not sexually liberating life.

As the car turns down yet another narrow and cobblestoned street, I glance down to the address written on the scrap of paper my father handed me, crinkled and damp now from the sweatiness of my palm.

I'm nervous. Of course, I am. I'm in a foreign country I've never visited, I'm heading to meet a jewel fence I've never met, and this is the first and last big job for my father. And I can't screw it up.

The car slows and pulls up next to a Gothic-style building, with a gray polished stone and brick exterior taking up much of the block. I smoosh my face to the side against the window, looking up. at the magnitude of the building's façade.

Spires adorn the ends of the building, reaching up toward the sky as if trying to touch the heavens. Gargoyles sit poised atop dormered window ledges, adding a dark and foreboding presence.

"Here we are, darling," Dorian's voice breaks the silence and the whirl of self-doubt flitting through my brain. "Doesn't look much like what I'd pictured your grandmother's house to look like. Are you sure this is the right place? I think this is a nightclub."

My smile is meant to reassure her. When I'd made up the story to appease Dorian's curiosity, I kept with the details Mudd had given me. I told her she'd be dropping me off at my grandmother's address. However, looking at the building, and Dorian's knowledge of the place, I now realize my mistake. Because this is clearly not a house. Not even an apartment building.

It's definitely a nightclub.

I look back out the window and shrug, the lie rolling effort-lessly off my tongue.

"Oh, yeah, well I was going to go to my grandmother's house, but since it's late and my grandmother is asleep, I'm meeting my cousin here first. He works here."

Dorian squints underneath her false eyelashes, giving me a dubious stare but doesn't question me. Why should she? And why should she even care?

Knocking on the driver's glass barrier, she signals the driver who comes around the car to open my door and extract my bag from the trunk.

Suddenly my nerves dance, as if someone turned the volume up to high on some Techno-pop dance groove. I have no idea what, or rather, who awaits me once I step out of the safety of this car and into the ominous building.

I'm like a blind rat following a trail of cheese, with the only instructions provided to me being this address and a name. A code name I am to use as a way of introduction.

Jersey.

Using this code name will signal my arrival to the fence for the meeting my father arranged. I don't know who the fence is, whether they are male or female, or even who I'm to ask for. It's all very cloak and dagger, which I'm sure my father structured that way on purpose.

He doesn't trust you.

Which is fine, and nothing I can change now, but it certainly makes it more complex. But it's just a means to an end. A well-engineered process for completing the job. Get in and out and return home with the satisfaction of knowing I accomplished the goal and I can leave with my freedom intact.

Dorian rests her hand gently on my wrist and gives me a quick, almost motherly squeeze. I nearly flinch at the contact, but my focus is redirected as she removes something out of her Hermès wallet and places it in my upturned palm.

"Darling, if you need anything while you're here, I'm staying at the Grand Plaza Hotel. Don't hesitate to call me. I'm happy to help."

I look down at the card and at the diamonds on her fingers and her bracelets. For a split second, I consider doing what I've been taught to do all my life. To swipe those rings right off her long, manicured hands without notice. I could do it so easily, just like I switched out the contraband in her purse. It's amazing how a little redirection can open up opportunities.

But the thought of doing it to Dorian makes me queasy. She's been a sweet and helpful asset, and regardless of the fact I'll never see her again, I hate the thought of damaging that trust. Even if those rings are probably worth a fortune and she wouldn't even miss them.

I smile sweetly, thanking her profusely for the ride, as I lean in to kiss her on both cheeks the European style I've seen on TV, before getting out of the car.

"Thank you, Dorian. I'll definitely call if I need anything."

Closing the door with a quiet snick of the latch, I turn to find the driver handing me my meager belongings.

"Thanks," I acknowledge, unceremoniously throwing the backpack over my shoulder and staring at the building in front of me.

He grunts, turning around and skirting around the hood of the car, as Dorian rolls down the window, a warning tone in her voice.

"Be careful, darling. Nothing good ever happens here late at night for a young girl. If I were you, I'd rethink this and go back to where you came from before it's too late."

Her comment is like a bucket of cold ice water thrown over my head, sending chills down my back. But before I'm able to say anything else, the window closes, the tint hiding her face inside.

As the car drives off, I'm left to respond to only passerbys. "I wish it were that easy."

CHAPTER 3

As I step inside the large, looming 16th century archway, my senses are assaulted with the loud cacophony of sounds, smells and the sight of strobe lights flashing in time to the techno beat. The music thumps and pounds off a base beat so strong I can feel it in my own bodily vibrations.

Club goers mill about, as I search the room for someone who looks like they expect me. My gaze sweeps across the large, open expanse, landing on the shape of a man standing high above the club's floor, his hands gripping the railing, as he casually surveys his surroundings like a king measuring the depths of his kingdom.

His posture is stiff. Guarded. Purposeful.

His profile comes into view as he twists, speaking to someone who is at his side. I notice the clench of his jaw, tight and menacing. A jaw that looks like it's been etched from marble and formed by an artist's hand. A nose sculpted and regal, not overly long or crooked, but with enough character to know it's not perfectly untouched.

He continues to scan over the crowd, listening to the person next to him, until his gaze reaches mine. It locks in on me like a dark, sinister tractor beam, pinning me down and sucking me in.

I can't tell the color of his eyes from this distance, but I know they're dark and piercing. They hold dark secrets that may never see the light of day. Those eyes aren't the eyes of a man who asks questions. They get their answers and what they need through control.

It gives me both a shiver of thrill and fissure of fear.

The connection is palpable, his gaze penetrating me. Like a sharp object slicing through my skin and boring into the very depths of my soul. His stare is so intense that it burrows under the layers of my skin until it hits the very core deep inside me, splits me open, and bubbles up to the surface.

MY BLOOD BOILS thick like hot lava, rushing to the very tips of my fingers and flesh. The way he stares at me has me wanting to relinquish control of everything - my thoughts, my body and my soul – and give it all to him without protest.

His gaze hasn't altered, but I finally break the connection when I'm startled by the soft, distinctly female voice next to me.

"May I help you, miss?"

There's a strong foreign accent filtering through her English. Maybe French or Dutch, I can't tell which, but I know I've never heard anything quite as elegant.

As I twist around, I find a beautiful and exquisite hostess wearing a short, tight black lace dress, at least four-inch heels and her long white-blonde hair intricately braided around the crown of her head.

I feel incredibly inadequate and frumpy next to this woman in my grey cargo pants, white off-the-shoulder sweater, and Chucks.

I can barely even hear myself speak over the music. "Oh, yes. I'm not sure if I'm in the right place or not…"

My throat is scratchy, and I cough. "But I was told to um, meet Jersey. Or, I mean, I'm Jersey. Or, shit…"

The woman, who can't be more than a few years older than me, lifts her brows in amusement, looking perplexed, but smiles softly and presses a few buttons on her tablet she holds in her hand.

"Jersey?" she repeats with a quirk of her head, and I nod.

She taps in the code name and then says, "One moment, s'il vous plait."

Ah, French.

It makes everything sound so much more pleasing and unearths a sadness in me that I didn't continue my foreign language studies in high school. It's such a beautiful and elegant language, but due to my other "studies" that my father had me doing after school, I never got to spend time learning it, only a few basic terms.

The woman taps an earpiece in her ear, a blinking blue light I hadn't noticed before, and she speaks. "Oui. I have a guest here who says she's here for someone named Jersey. Or," she flicks a glance at me. "Is Jersey. She doesn't know."

There's a pause and she nods her head. "Yes, but…"

It's apparent she's been cut off by whoever is on the other end, and she opens and closes her mouth, saying nothing.

"Mm-hmm. Oui. D'accord. Oui. Merci, monsieur."

She ends the conversation and the blue light disappears as she turns her head and smiles.

"One moment, miss. Someone will be down momentarily. May I take your bag?"

I scrunch my nose and give a quick jerk of my shoulder away from her, gripping the strap tight in my hands. "No," I snap, ridiculously flustered. "That's okay. I've got it."

A group of young people – mostly women in short dresses and high heels – walk through the doors and the hostess turns her attention to them as I slink back into the shrouded darkness of the wall. Hiding in the shadows, not at all inconspicuous, wondering what the hell comes next.

Not more than five minutes pass, and a large black man in a sleek royal blue suit that clings to his enormous bulk approaches, stopping just shy of a foot in front of me. Towering over me like a Redwood in a forest of pine needles. Because of his sheer size and the fact he didn't provide me a name, I've labeled him Hulk. Seems fitting.

"Come with me."

He abruptly turns and begins walking down a dark corridor, illuminated only by the track lighting lining the walls just inches above the floor.

A little dazed from his curt behavior, and probably mildly jet lagged, I clutch my bag and rush to catch up nearly tripping at his heels when he stops at an elevator that is hidden so discreetly into the wall, I wouldn't have even known it was there. He enters a code into a panel, blocking the keypad from my view with his hulking form.

The door opens without a sound and Hulk steps in, keeping his back to me. I follow closely behind, leaving enough space for my comfort, and enter the lift as I feel the whoosh of the metal doors closing behind me. I'm suddenly overwhelmed by the magnitude of what I'm doing and where I'm at. I have no idea who these people are or if I'm safe.

I wouldn't put it past my father to send me into the lion's den. He's never really had my best interests at heart.

Mr. Hulk doesn't turn around and remains facing the opposite set of doors which soon open, and we step into a quiet, even darker corridor. There's no club thumping or music beats up on this level. Just the sounds of my sharp intakes of breath and the rubbery squeaks of my shoe soles on the floor filling in the stillness of the hallway.

The man stops and turns at a doorway but doesn't look at me. He simply says, "Wait here."

And I do. What else am I supposed to do? I have no idea where I'm at, much less who I'm supposed to be waiting for, but I do as he says, anxious for what comes next.

As he disappears through the door, every nuance of this job finally comes into clear view, like I'm looking through a magnifying glass and it's just come into focus on that small, infinitesimal subject that finally turns into something recognizable.

I'm both significant and insignificant in the grand scheme of things. Both necessary and unnecessary. I'm just a conduit and a wheel in a cog. The mule to bring this deal to fruition.

I'm inconsequential to whoever is behind that door awaiting my arrival. In a matter of minutes, I'll finish this job and be on my way.

But all the secrecy has me curious. Is this what all my dad's jobs are like? Code words and dark interiors?

I guess I understand it to an extent since this is an illegal transaction and I am in possession of a stolen jewel. I have no clue how Mudd wound up with this stone or what the bidding process looked like, and how he settled on a buyer, but it doesn't matter to me now.

It's just weird, in my opinion, to meet the buyer at a club. I thought I'd conclude the deal with the fence someplace else. Like in the jewelry district. It's confusing to be in such a different environment from what I expected.

Spinning around, there's a bank of tinted windows behind me, and I step up to the glass, looking down over the crowd below. Sex is in the air, infiltrating the rhythm of the music as dancers grind and move seductively together, their bodies fluid, a beautiful ribbon of motion.

To my left is the spot where I saw that man standing a while ago, but who is now gone. I scan the area again in case I can spot him again.

But before I can locate him, the door creaks open, a flash of golden light shining across the floor, as the scent of tobacco and bourbon seeping out along with the arc of light streaming over the darkness.

I inhale deeply, the deliciously warm scent filling my nostrils and giving me confidence.

"He'll see you now."

CHAPTER 4

My feet don't take me more than a step inside the doorway when someone moves in from behind me, encroaching on my space and blocking my exit.

Fear sparks inside my heart, and on instinct, I try to use my bag as a weapon to disarm and throw him off, but my actions are thwarted as Hulk's large hands grip my biceps, whipping my bag from my shoulder and binding my wrists together in one fell swoop.

I try to turn my head to see what the hell is going on and who is behind me when suddenly, I'm shoved from behind into Hulk's chest, my head yanked back forcefully by my hair and my scream muffled by a rough hand clamped over my mouth.

My vision is taken away from me when a hood, smelling distinctly like male musk and sweat, is thrown over my head, shrouding me in darkness.

I struggle to breathe, my anxiety and panic creating a whirlpool of fear cresting through me descending down my stomach, triggering the rise and swirl of bile up through my throat. I force myself to focus and breathe through my nose, in and out, and keep my shit together to avoid embarrassing myself.

My fight or flight instinct is great, but fighting is pointless against the massive rock in front of me and whoever is behind me, now using some plastic binder to cinch my wrists together, cutting into the sensitive flesh there. With my hands bound and my sight completely blocked out, I'm forced to my knees with a strong pair of hands on my shoulders.

Tears sting my eyes as I crumble to the floor in a heap, but I will myself to remain tough and resolute.

You're here to do a job. You can do this.

"Who the fuck are you?"

The voice. It's sharp as a knife and cuts through my panic that is now settling into a low simmer.

While the words are terse and meant to intimidate, the sound somehow has the opposite effect. The voice is very male, rich and radiates heat, sending tremors through the air and settling over me like an elixir to a sore throat.

It penetrates my fear and somehow bolsters my confidence. Challenges me to speak up and push out of this captive shell of mine.

But as I fumble to find my voice through my parched throat, the voice barks at me again.

"You're not fucking Mudd. So, I ask again. Who are you?"

My voice trembles and betrays me. "I'm his daughter. Mudd sent me to deliver the product."

There's some shuffling nearby, and while I'm still completely blinded, my head moves toward the direction of the sound. Two pairs of shoes tread over the floor to my right. And in front of me, the man's voice. Close.

"Here you go, boss." It's Hulk's voice.

It's the sound of a zipper and my bag being opened. My backpack. They're looking through the contents of my backpack.

There's a low murmur and grunt.

"Gemma Lynn Phillips. Born February 16, 1999. 3416 Washington Street, Hoboken, New Jersey."

Silence.

There's a faint tapping noise, as if the man asking me the questions is thrumming my plastic driver's license against something hard in an inpatient manner. As if he's thinking or waiting for some revelation.

"Tell me, Gem-*ma*," he says, extending the syllables in my name to punctuate the end. "Why is it that I have the twenty-year-old daughter of Mudd Phillips in front of me, who looks like she should be in a college classroom instead of this club, and not her father? Hmm?"

Suddenly, I'm blinking past the flood of brightness emitting through the room as the hood is whipped off my head and the room – and people in it – are revealed to me.

I scan the room quickly, noticing Hulk and another man, just as large, standing off to the side, and then the man who is obviously in charge and grilling me in front of me. And then I carefully assess my exits, developing an exit strategy should I have the chance to take it.

My observations aren't covert enough, however, because the man snicks out an amused laugh.

"Give up that idea, little girl. There is no way out unless I *let* you out."

Flicking my attention back to the man now sitting at a desk in front of me, I notice several things all at once.

Where Hulk is big and burly, this man is sleek and lean under a dark, tailored suit. From what I can tell, he is a little over average height, maybe six-foot, with strong, broad shoulders that pull back into a posture that is cultured and refined. As if he was reminded as a child to sit up straight and not slouch.

He sits back against a leather-back chair, the black wool of his suit draped in a tapered fashion to fit snugly against his chest and torso. Tight enough to illustrate the well-maintained and toned muscles pronounced underneath. A crisp white shirt is adorned by a bright azure colored tie that is knotted so tight I wonder how he can even breathe.

My eyes track upward as he slowly stands again, and moves out from behind the desk, and then my gaze lowers to the manner in which his slacks highlight his toned legs – runner, perhaps? – and the thick asset cupped between his legs.

I may have never seen one up close and personal before, but I know a well-endowed man when I see one.

He stands patiently, as if waiting for me to get my fill, hands crossed over his chest, head tilted to the side, his shrewd, whisky-brown eyes taking me in with a scowl etched across his full mouth. He looks at me with contempt. As if I've ruined his entire night with my arrival.

But his displeasure isn't like the one I fear from my father. This man, although wound tight, doesn't seem ready to strike out in violence or drunken abuse, like I've seen happen with Mudd on more occasions than I can count.

This man, his temper hidden just under the surface, but still visible through the vein in his neck that's corded tight and the clench of his closely cropped beard across his jawline, keeps his emotions in check. He's guarded, controlled, and clearly in charge.

The same man I saw earlier.

I clear my throat and wiggle upright to offer a less submissive position, even though I'm still on my knees with my hands bound behind my back.

"I'm here on Mudd's behalf to make the exchange. I've brought what you want and once I get what we're owed, I'll leave."

He clicks his tongue against his teeth and *tsks*.

"You'll just leave, will you?" He takes several steps forward to close the distance between us, and I drop my eyes to the floor and brace for what's to come.

Will he hit me? Knock me unconscious?

I have no way to defend myself except to suck in a deep breath and wait for pain to come. His scent – a warm masculinity mixed with leather and expensive cologne – fills the air in my nostrils, making me flush with anticipation.

But instead, as I stare down at the shiny points of his black shoes just in front of my knees, my shoulders quivering lightly, all I feel is the light touch of his fingers as they slip through my hair, over the shell of my ear and down my neck.

I shiver at the contact.

I've never been touched this way before. It's sensual, not compassionate. Erotic yet with a hint of violence. I remain still, apprehensive to his intentions, but my eyes automatically close at the sensation. The soft strokes of his fingers across my skin and along my collarbone send ripples of fire through my blood and swims up my spine.

I clench my thighs together as the progression of his touch moves lower, tracing the edge of my shirt that angles over my chest, my left shoulder exposed by the style of my blouse.

His voice is rough. "You don't go until I allow it. Until the deal is done. Until I have confirmed the authenticity and purity of the gem. In the meantime, I might have something else in mind for you, considering your presence altered my plans entirely."

I blink up at him, my eyes watering when he fists my hair in his hand, and he tugs my head back to look at him.

"Ahh," I cry out, more in shock rather than pain, a gust of air whooshing from my lungs, my lips falling open on the exhale.

He seems emboldened by my response because the corner of his lips curls up into a smirk, and he groans deeply before letting me go with such force that I lose my balance and wobble to my elbows before regaining my equilibrium.

The man turns abruptly toward the desk, his back to me, lifting the bag and dumping it out, the contents spilling out over the mahogany.

"Where is it, Gemma?" His words are punched into the air and punctuated like keys on a keyboard. "Where is my diamond that I was promised?"

"It's hidden in a safe place."

His head snaps back around and he gives a brisk nod to Hulk, who is at my side instantly, a large hand slipping underneath my armpit and jerking me to my feet.

"Where is it hidden? Don't you dare fuck with me, little girl."

It's only then that a ribbon of fear lashes through me, even though at this moment I have the upper hand.

I bite down on my lip and smile coyly as the man faces me, annoyance written all over his handsome, cold features.

"Inside me."

CHAPTER 5

Technically, I didn't swallow the jewel or shove it anywhere inside any of my bodily orifices.

I did, however, hide it in a small leather pouch, which I slipped into my panties and between my thighs earlier in the dark corridor while I waited.

THE ADMISSION DOES little to quell the anger that registers first as shock on the man's face but transforms quickly into something akin to piqued interest.

He strides with purposeful steps back to me, his body so close that I have to tilt my head back to look him in the eye.

It's there in his eyes when I see exactly what he's about to do.

I'm his conquest. He'll take what he wants no matter the obstacle or what pitiful resistance I try to offer.

"Give it to me now," he demands, his palm out to prove his seriousness. "Or I will get it myself."

I don't know why I feel like digging my heels in at this moment. I should just get it over with, the sooner the better so he can run his tests, and I can take the money and run. Maybe it's my stubborn rebellion that's been kept hidden from my father all these years, cowering in the closet until now. Why I've decided to bring it out now or for this man is completely illogical.

Or, it's simple stupidity.

This man could hurt me. Could end me right here, and no one would ever know. I mean, my dad knows I'm here, but I have little faith that he would give a shit if I ever came home. He would, however, care about his profitable loss.

Yet, still, I resist.

And that's all it takes. One moment of clever disobedience and he proves exactly what he means. What he's capable of doing. Who he is and who I am not.

A puff of air escapes my lips when his firm hand darts behind my neck and tightly grasps the nape, holding me in place – locking me in and leaving me immobile – while the other hand jams roughly down the front of my pants.

It's shocking the amount of force he uses, yet his face remains extremely calm, only a twitch of his lip and an eyebrow that quirks up, as if to say, *"Don't play games with me, little girl. You won't win."*

I nearly jump out of my skin from the contact as his fingers push through the barrier of my pantie's edge, and his knuckles graze over my neatly trimmed pussy. A place no one has ever touched me.

It's jarring and exhilarating at the same time. This man wields his power over me, demonstrating the lengths he will go to prove he is in control and will get what he wants no matter the cost. I should be scared shitless and utterly disgusted by his dominant display of control.

Yet, I'm not the least bit frightened.

Because the look in his eye as his fingers brush over the warmth of my center tells me everything I need to know.

This excites him, too.

Even though he's trying to hide his outward reaction, he can't hide the sudden change in the rhythm of his breaths and the pulse that *thumps* chaotically in the vein in his neck.

Thump, thump thump, thump.

Our eyes lock as his fingers locate the small, velvet pouch. He latches it in a fist and drags it purposefully across my center, the bag's plush material tormenting me with the suggestive nature of the action. My body's physical reaction is immediate and embarrassingly carnal.

The touch isn't long enough as he swiftly removes his hand, staring down at the small bag in his palm. I'm frozen and stat-uesque as I gaze at him, curious as to what he'll do now that he has what he wants.

Slowly, methodically, he lifts the bag to his nose, as my eyes grow wild with an animalistic bewilderment, and he takes in a long inhale. His lids close, his lips parting slightly, and the length of his dark lashes practically reach the top of his cheekbones.

He speaks through closed eyelids, his voice a low growl. "Fuck me. You just made this arrangement all the more valuable."

I don't understand what his comment means, so I cock my head to the side in confusion as his brown eyes open again fully. But now instead of anger, they are filtered with something dark and licentious.

Lust isn't something new to me or anything I'm unaccustomed to seeing in men, as I've been the target of many leering stares since I hit puberty and developed a curvaceous body. I have what is referred to as an "exotic" look.

My mother was Brazilian, and it seems my curves, starting with my well-endowed breasts accentuate my small waistline and full hips, come directly from her voluptuous side of the family. My light olive-colored skin is smooth, highlighting my tanned, long giraffe legs that were gangly looking until I turned sixteen, when they somehow overnight turned shapely, leading up to my full, round bottom.

I'm not a stranger to fending off men who have made their attempts to touch and grope my ass and boobs over the years, who tell me how sexy and beautiful I am, in hopes that their words will be the key to unlocking my legs for them.

But I've kept them firmly and resolutely closed.

And once I've denied any reciprocal interest in them, shooting down their efforts to get me on my back, that desire for me sours, turning into slimy, misogynistic harassment, their once complimentary language growing sordid and ugly.

Slut. Whore. Cock-tease. Prude. Bitch.

You name it, I've been called it. The worst offenders happened to be my own father and brother.

My best revenge happened to be holding myself above their contempt by keeping my body pure. I've never allowed a boy or a man to touch me. I've worked hard to downplay my appearance by avoiding tight or revealing clothing, often-times putting on my brother's flannel shirts to cover my figure.

So, to experience this electrifying sensation that registers deep within my loins from this man's touch, and noticing his visible reaction to me, alters my opinion on sexual attraction.

I don't know who this man is, only that he's the fence brought in to purchase this stolen diamond. The contact for which we exchange product for money to satisfy the prearranged agreement.

But I want to know him. And I don't want this conversation to be over so quickly. So, I ask the question that's on my mind. The one I want answered.

"What's more valuable than what's in your hand?" My voice is basically a trace of whisper.

His tongue darts out to lick his bottom lip before he stuffs it back in his cheek with a crooked grin.

"*You*, Gemma. You just raised the stakes in this deal."

CHAPTER 6

W ith the jut of his chin, he orders Hulk over to my side, who grasps my bicep in his large hand.

"Dempsey, take her back to the Cove and then call Roman and West. Tell them I'll be by later after I run the authenticity tests at the shop."

"Yes, boss."

The "boss" gives me a pointed look, narrowing his eyes into slits so all I see is a pool of dark through his lashes.

He pinches my chin between his thumb and index finger, hard, swiveling my head side-to-side before dropping it harshly.

"If you're conning me, Gemma Phillips, you will pay. Your father will pay. I am not a man you fuck with. Do you understand what I'm telling you?"

I stutter. "*I-I'm* not…we're not trying to fuck with you. I promise."

He huffs out a sarcastic laugh. "The word of a twenty-year old jewel thief? Is that an oxymoron?"

Everything in me wants to argue. To riot against his sarcasm and mistrust. But it's difficult to do when he steps in close again, his solid chest pushing against my breasts. It's threatening and meant to intimidate, but it's sexually thrilling, and it makes my panties go damp.

All I can imagine is what it would feel like if the clothes between us disappeared and his body covered mine, entering me for the first time. Taking my virginity and filling me with his cock.

I lift a shoulder in a half shrug, biting down on my lip to stop the quivering. Whether it's from fear or lust, I can't quite determine.

"My word is good," I say with more confidence than I feel. "I wouldn't be here in person making this deal if that weren't the case."

He considers this for a moment and then tips his head in a nod, signaling Hulk to do his bidding. As I'm ushered away by the grip of Hulk's hold, I'm led out a door that isn't the one we entered. I twist in his grasp, looking back at the man whose name I still don't know to find him staring at my retreating form.

"Wait…you can't do this. Just let me call my father. You can't just kidnap me like this!"

The sound of my voice is sheer panic, risen to a level of delirium. With my hands still tied behind my back, there's nothing I can do to protect myself from whatever nefarious plan he has to keep me.

Our eyes connect again, mine pleading for help from a man who has no intention of helping me. Without a word, he lifts the pouch again to his nose, his eyes blazing a dark need.

"Don't worry, little girl. If what you say is true, and the product you've brought is legitimate, then you'll be free to return to your home a day from now." He tilts his head, cocking a suspicious eyebrow. "But if you're lying and I don't get what I was promised, then there are other ways I will make you pay."

I may be a virgin, but his threat registers a spark of heat low in my belly, and I have to turn away, so he doesn't notice the flush that rises up my throat and neck like a vine, indicating the effect it has on me.

Because while his warning isn't explicit, I understand what it means. I'm not stupid in the ways of the world. I know what a man like him could do with a girl like me.

The worst-case scenario is he could sell me for a price, I suppose, to the highest bidder. Best case is…well, I don't know. And I don't want to find out.

"Please," I beg again. "Please just call Mudd and he'll clear up all this confusion. You don't have to hold me hostage to make that happen."

He moves toward me, Hulk holding my arms behind my back, leaving me vulnerable to anything this man might do. And because I'm prone to beatings, I flinch when he trails a finger down the side of my face.

"I'm afraid that's just not how this works, Gemma. You don't call the shots. Mudd has already changed the rules in our arrangement, and therefore he's broken my trust. So, until I confirm I haven't been duped, you're staying where I can monitor you. That means no phone, no contact, and no complaints. You'll do as I say or there will be consequences."

He flicks his wrist toward the door and once again, I'm being forced down a darkened stairwell until we hit a door that requires an entry code. Hulk stands to the side to block my view as he enters a 4-digit code and a door opens into a parking garage. Definitely not a public one from the handful of vehicles, all of expensive taste and quality.

Aston Martin. Maserati. Bentley.

Hulk rounds the hood of a dark-colored Tesla and opens the back door for me.

"Get in," he snarls, and I do as he says. There's no reason to argue with this man. I wouldn't win a fight with him, plus he's only doing what his boss has told him to do.

As he settles in the driver's seat, I decide to finally ask the question.

"What's his name? Your boss?"

I notice his eyes flicker from the rearview mirror. He gives a shake of his head and chuckles.

"Boss."

Rolling my eyes, I grumble like a schoolgirl. "Seriously? You know what I mean. How can I do business with a man when I can't even address him properly?"

He thinks for a moment and then lifts his brick of a shoulder. "If he wanted you to know his name, he would have introduced himself."

"Fine. I'll find out on my own."

"You do that."

ૐ

APPARENTLY, the Cove is the name of a condo building of some sort.

After Hulk parks in a private stall, we ride a private elevator up to the top floor – a sprawling labyrinth of a home, the likes of which I've never seen.

Opulence doesn't come close to describing this place. My home in Jersey could easily fit in the kitchen alone.

Hulk leads me through a hallway littered with works of art, some of which I've seen at the Met the one and only time I ever went there on a school field trip in middle school. If I had to put a price tag on any of these paintings, I'd say they'd sell for at least a half million or more.

I may not be an artist yet, nor do I appraise art, but that doesn't mean I'm not a good judge of rare collections. These pieces are worth some bank.

If this is where the man lives, he has invested a lot of money on fine-ass things. We walk a maze of hallways and finally end up at a locked door. Hulk produces a key, unlocks it and opens it up, pointing inside with a tilt of his head.

"Boss will be back soon. You're to stay here until he arrives."

"Oh goodie." I roll my eyes insolently.

He nudges me forward with a hefty finger at my shoulder blade, pushing me in. I stall a few feet inside, checking for any possible exits and wondering how the hell I was going to get out of the ties still binding my wrists.

I lift my hands behind my back, flailing like a roped calf at a rodeo.

"I haven't used the bathroom since before I left the airport today. I really need to pee and can't without the use of my hands. Unless you want to wipe my ass."

He grumbles and sighs, considering the verity of my request. Instead of a verbal response, he simply rummages through his front pants pocket, takes out a small tool, and unlocks the bindings that fall to the floor.

My wrists throb and fingers tingle from being bound and unable to move for that long, so I roll them around to restart the flow of blood supply.

"Thank you," I offer quietly.

My stomach rumbles just then, and it seems to echo across the cavernous room. "I'm really hungry, too. Can I get something to eat? I had some granola bars in my bag, but your boss kept that."

His face seems to soften just a little but then he seems to reconsider, the compassion disappearing in an instant.

"Don't know, don't care. Bathroom is over there," he points to the far side of the room, which I now see is just as luxurious as the rest of the apartment. "I'll see about some food."

He turns to go, my mind racing as I try to figure out a way out of this situation.

I don't know why my father put me in this position, but he damn well better make it right. And if this Boss guy doesn't see fit to let me go, I'll need to devise a plan of my own.

Because pickpocketing isn't my only skill.

I'm also a damn good lock picker.

CHAPTER 7

I can't be sure how long I've slept, but the last thing I remember after Hulk brought me some food and left me alone again was curling up on the large four-poster bed and then it was lights out.

With the cross-continental travel and time change, the stress over the meeting and the adrenaline rush of being kidnapped, I was exhausted, mind and body.

A loud commotion outside the door stirs me awake, my brain in a foggy state and far from clearheaded when I jump from the shouting. Voices of at least two men, maybe three irritated men, arguing over something.

Fear kicks in and starts to niggle at the bottom of my belly. I slide out of the bed, realizing I'm no longer wearing any shoes, which startles me further because I never removed them myself. At least, not that I recall.

A quick perusal of the rest of my body confirms that I'm still fully clothed, and I breathe a sigh of relief. I must've been out cold from the jetlag. Unless the food that was brought in was drugged.

I consider this possibility as I pad quietly over to the door and place my ear up to the wood grain. Although there's a chance something could've been slipped in my food, I don't feel lethargic or hungover, my head not swimming in thick confusion. I'm just tired.

The voices are now hushed, but loud enough that I can hear garbled portions of the conversation, identifying a few words from each response.

"...what the fuck...prisoner here? Faron, she's....a kid."

"West...remind you...she's in...con...Mudd...dirty work... daughter...I will not...beautiful girl...I want...promised me... use her as leverage."

Staggering back a few steps, my hand instinctively covers my mouth on a gasp.

What has my dad done? Did he screw this guy over, along with me, by not delivering what was promised? But why? What would motivate him to do something like that?

I pace back and forth as the men continue talking. But I've given up trying to hear them clearly. They must be in a closed room down the hall so it's frustrating only obtaining a few words at a time and trying to make sense of them. But what I have heard has given me enough insight to know I'm in trouble.

Big, *big* trouble, unless I can find a way out of this mess. Unfortunately, I don't know how I can do that and until I do, I'm stuck.

Literally, I'm a sitting duck.

I check the latch on the large window once again and find it won't budge. Banging on it or screaming for help is useless because I'm too high from the ground and no one could hear my cries for help, anyway.

With my back toward the door from my perch at the windowsill, the snick of the lock and the door opening behind me causes me to stiffen up. I remain still, counting to ten, breathing in and out, knowing I need to keep my composure and remain in control.

Although I will myself not to move, my body still reacts wildly the minute he places a dominating hand on my shoulder. I jump with a startled scream as he captures my arms, pinning them to my sides and spinning me around to face him.

It has only been a few hours since I last felt the intensity of his dark eyes boring through me, but now up close in the small confines of this room, they burn darker than before, coal-colored and fuming. As if they had been on fire, the embers now smoldering from whatever has caused his agitation.

He drops my arms as we lock eyes in a battle of wills. My posture suggests I won't cower, even though inside I'm scared shitless. I remain silent, waiting for him to say something.

"What the fuck are you trying to pull here, Gemma? Did you not think I'd find out?"

My mouth drops open incredulously.

"*I*-I don't know what you mean." I shake my head, suddenly feeling a lightheaded wooziness descending over me.

He glowers as a hostile laugh leaves his mouth, his eyes flashing with annoyance. "Playing the innocent card won't let you off the hook with me, beautiful. I won't fall for that."

"First of all..." I stop midsentence because I want to address him by his name, yet I still don't know it. "What the hell is your name? All I know is that Hulk calls you Boss."

My redirection seems to confuse him, as his tight mouth slowly loosens and curves up slightly at the corners for a second, snickering a deep and throaty sound. "Who the fuck is Hulk?"

I shrug, flapping my hand toward the doorway. "You know, the big guy. The bodyguard or whoever he is that does your dirty work. Seems fitting, if you ask me."

Boss nods appreciatively. "Yes, it does. As for me, you can call me Faron."

Through an exaggerated cough, he adds, "Or *Sir* when you're on your knees."

Lifting a brow at the suggestive tone, I scoff. "I'll stick with Faron."

He pauses, arching his own eyebrow in question. "I guess I assumed your father would have mentioned my name as your contact."

Averting my eyes away, I cross my arms to prove my frustration. "You'd think so, but that isn't the case. I was given as little detail as possible, probably because my dad..."

He prompts me with the cock of his head. "Your dad, what?"

"He doesn't trust me. Or rather, he doesn't trust anyone, for that matter. But he kept things vague on purpose, probably knowing I would object if I knew he was trying to scam you."

Faron considers this bit of information, nodding his head reluctantly.

"So you're saying you didn't know you were carrying a fake?"

His eyes bore into me with such intensity, flashing darkly as they roam over me, that my nipples tighten in response. Inexplicably, my panties dampen between my legs, a pulsing heat forming low in my belly.

Faron, in all his broody bluster, has an effect on me. My body seems to have awoken like the snowy white princess in the fairytale. But he's certainly not a Prince Charming. More like a Prince of Darkness.

"Listen, *Faron*," I enunciate clearly. "Like I said, I had no idea who you even were, or that I brought a fake. All I know is what Mudd told me. He gave me your address, the code word and gave me strict instructions to give the diamond only to you and no one else. That's it."

He taps a long finger against his lips, a silver ring glinting off the band.

"Then I can only conclude your father did a bait-and-switch, with both the delivery method" – he gestures between us at me – "and the product."

I crinkle my nose and forehead. "I don't know what motive Mudd has to send me with a fake. Why would he do it?"

"Excellent question. And if he'd return my call, maybe we'd find out."

I'm about to suggest that I should try to call him when he reaches up and strokes my cheek with a rough thumb. It's clearly not meant to be gentle.

It's meant to suggest whatever he decides to do, I'm part of his plan to get what he wants out of Mudd.

"And what, little girl, shall I do with *you in the meantime.*"

CHAPTER 8

The entire atmosphere changes as he leaves the room, presumably to ruminate over his options, as I remain locked behind closed doors. It had been charged and electric as he stood close, towering over me, touching my face with his thumb.

And now I feel cold and alone, wanting to be the object of his attention again. And for him to call me little girl.

I should be offended by the way he keeps calling me little girl, which is indecently patronizing. But in some weird way, I like it because of its suggestive connotation.

And frankly, it reminds me of who he is and who I am not. And I like that power dichotomy.

Technically, I'm not his equal. Far from it. I'm naïve in this world where he's had years of experience. And his knowledge of this business gives him insight into the reasons behind Mudd's motives for doing this and why my father sent me and not someone else.

My father could have sent any of his underlings. Men with far more practice and familiarity in this type of transaction.

When Mudd assigned me to this deal, he said it was to keep things on the downlow. That no one would look twice at me flying to Europe. It would keep the Feds off our scent. Mudd couldn't afford to attract any more attention to his wheeling and dealings because he was already going through a trial for extortion and various other federal crimes.

The logic seemed reasonable to me at the time. But now I'm questioning everything he said to me before I left, rewinding every conversation leading up to my departure and peeling back the onion layer strip by strip to figure out what he has up his sleeve.

But nothing is clear to me, and I've not come to any conclusion.

Before Faron left, I'd suggested he let me call Mudd directly to see if I could get him to come clean about the product. Considering my father's nickname, coming clean is obviously an oxymoron. Mudd is as dirty as they come.

Regardless, my father owes me an explanation and I want to know why he did this to me. My father has never loved me, and he treated me with the same care as he would anything he owned and managed. But I was mistaken when I thought he'd given me this opportunity because it meant he trusted me and had faith that I'd come through for him.

Instead, he put me in a dangerously compromising position. One that could jeopardize my safety if Faron sees fit to hurt me. He's technically already kidnapped me and holds me prisoner against my will. What's to say he won't dispose of me if I don't get him what he wants?

I pace the room, running everything through my head as I notice my beautiful surroundings. The silk of the comforter over the massive king-size bed, the rumpled sheets where I'd fallen asleep. There are certainly worse places I could be held captive, and the accommodations here are far better than anything I've ever slept in before.

Aside from the handcuffs and unnecessary hooded cover, I haven't been mistreated in any way. And both of those restraints were promptly removed. I've been fed and given water, and Faron even said he'd send for some new clothes to be sent up for later. Every possible creature comfort I could desire was provided to me. And on the plus side, I'm as far away as possible from the man I call my father.

My hope is that once this matter is resolved and the deal is complete, I can return home and begin a new life out from under Mudd's thumb. With the promise that I'll be free from him and all the sorted, criminal elements associated with this family and life.

First things first, though. In order to be a free woman back home, I have to gain my freedom from Faron.

THE TOUCH IS FEATHER SOFT, gliding over my cheek as a cloud whispers through the sky. I lean into it, pressing my face closer to its warmth, a sigh passing through my lips to acknowledge my gratitude.

My heart begins to race, pulse quickening with every velvety touch. My limbs quiver as the touch lowers, tracing petals of indulgence over my skin, making its way over my collarbone. My sigh turns to raspy moans, my breasts heavy with need as

SIERRA HILL

the agile finger outlines the shape of my breast before flicking over a hardened nipple.

The craving to be touched is so great that my body instinctively moves into it, reaching like a flower to the sun. I flip onto my back, allowing for more area to explore...wanting the caress to continue wherever it's willing to go.

Like a math equation that's found its answer in the sum of its parts, my body yearns to be filled and completed by this roaming hand. To make me whole. To complete the puzzle with the missing piece.

The greedy desire manifests itself in a drenched wetness between my legs, the throbbing ache that begs to be satisfied in a way it's never known.

Touch me, touch me, touch me.

Is that my voice? My needy voice spoken through dry lips and a parched mouth? A husky desire vocalized into the darkness?

"Yes," I plea, as the touch finds its way over the swell of my belly, floating further until it hovers between my legs.

The heat from the hand penetrates the material of my panties, as I burn with excitement. It's so hot in here, like a furnace burning me up. The touch stops, and it's torture to be refused like this.

"Please."

I struggle to move, as something pins me in place, but I punch my hips forward, desperate to reach that elusive connection. But it vanishes and vaporizes in an instant and in a panic, my eyes fly open...

As if stepping out of a fog into bright light, I squint, blinking several times as I gain hold of reality. Was I dreaming? Did I fall asleep and have the most erotic dream of my life?

The room is dark and drafty, the covers thrown off my legs where tingles still linger between my thighs. I dare a glance down the bed and notice my legs are spread apart, my panties still damp, and my shirt rucked up to expose my belly.

But that's not the most startling aspect of this scene.

What's far more frightening, and arousing, is to find Faron standing at the edge of the bed, watching me through lowered lashes.

I scramble up the bed, moving swiftly to a sitting position, fumbling with the sheet to cover myself to avoid any further embarrassment.

"Did you have a good night sleep?" His voice is flat and stretched tight, but there's inflection in his tone that resembles amusement.

"Um, yes. I think. Were you…how long have you been standing there?"

He looks down at his chest, plucking at a piece of lint from his gray sweater, the contour of his biceps shaped solidly against the material. I'm somehow delighted and enthralled by the flex of his masculinity.

"Long enough to enjoy it."

A crease forms in my brows.

"What does that mean?"

He stifles a laugh. "It means, I like the way you beg."

Oh. My. God.

The humiliation swallows me whole, and I sink back down and duck my head under the sheet to hide from his scrutiny. But no sooner is my embarrassment hidden when the cover is ripped from my hands and I'm exposed once again.

"I spoke with your father."

I check the clock on the nightstand to see what time it is and how long I've been out. It's after four p.m. here, which means I've slept over fifteen hours and it's mid-morning back in Jersey.

Faron sits at the edge of the bed near my hip.

"I've been in this business since before my father's death. Over twelve years now and I've met and worked with some pretty despicable associates in my time. Slimy, shady criminals. Men who would do just about anything for money," he says, running a hand over his chin stubble. He's close enough for me to reach out and touch him, but he's untouchable.

He continues. "But never in my career have I encountered someone like your father."

His gaze lands on me – sympathetic, but mostly pity. I glance away, ashamed by my upbringing. Cursing the blood that runs through my veins and the family I was born into.

I cringe. "Yeah, he's not a nice man."

"I should have listened to the rumors about his reputation. But I was greedy, and I wanted that diamond, so I gave into his demands and thought we negotiated a pretty damn good deal."

He looks off thoughtfully into the distance. "Not only has he reneged on his end by sending you with a counterfeit diamond, but he's changed the terms and is now demanding a higher asking price."

I stammer with my words, incredulous, yet not surprised by my father's deceit.

"But you told him you're holding me until he sends you what he promised?"

Faron clenches his jaw, pursing his lips in an angry glower, the dark stubble over his lips and chin joining in response.

"Indeed, I have. And his bargaining chip and part of this new price increase is actually *you*."

He scans my face waiting for a response to this claim. But all I have is confusion.

"I...I don't follow."

He chuckles humorlessly. Ominous to a cynical degree.

"Hmm...that says a lot about your, shall we say, inexperience."

Yes, I'm inexperienced in this business, but it shouldn't be to my father's benefit. Why would it be? What does that give him as an advantage in this situation?

"Um, okay. What did he say?"

Faron crosses his arms over his chest, one hand scrubbing over his scruff. I notice his stance, his long, tapered legs hip width apart, the strength clear underneath the tailored material and fit.

"He sold you. Or rather, he offered me your virginity as an incentive to finalize this deal."

CHAPTER 9

"He did what?"

My jaw drops, the room shifting and blurring as I try to come to terms with what Faron just said. An acute and very sharp pain stabs me in the middle of my chest. A knife being jammed in and then slowly removed by the audacity of my father's actions.

Mudd Phillips has never disguised his dislike of me since the day I was born and as long as I can remember. I wasn't the second son he wanted, and I drove my mother away, according to him. I was a nuisance, an annoying female complication that he couldn't figure out how to use to his advantage.

Yet, once I hit puberty, his entire outlook changed. When Mudd was sober, he drilled into me the importance of keeping myself pure because he didn't want to raise a grand-child. And when he was drunk, he would do a one-eighty, calling me names and slut-shaming me just for being a woman.

I ignored all of it because I had no desire to be any of those vile names he'd labeled me so cruelly and so often. I believed my virginity was the one and only thing I truly owned and had control over, so I protected it with everything I had.

Whereas every other aspect in my life was managed and controlled by Mudd. He dictated when I ate, what I ate, where I went, who I went with, when I would or would not attend school, where I lived, who my friends were, and what I would do to contribute to the family business.

In essence, I wasn't his daughter. I was his servant.

But this time? This time, it isn't just names. This time, he's created some sick game with my life, sending me on a mission to fence a fake diamond, and then disrupts the entire scheme by changing the rules.

Mudd has what Faron wants - the diamond – still in his possession, and Faron has the money to pay for it. And now I possess something of value, that has been factored into this crazy, convoluted equation.

I GROWL ANGRILY, jumping out from the warm comfort of the bed to pick up the pile of clean clothes Faron hands me.

"He has no right to give what doesn't belong to him."

Faron tilts his head, an arrogant smirk painted on his face. "Maybe. Maybe not. But it could've easily been mine for the taking ten minutes ago. Your body seemed ready to willingly offer it up to me."

I stop in my tracks on my way to the bathroom, spinning around to stare at him wide-eyed at how casually he just threw that out there.

He steps in toward me, prompting me to stare up into his dark cavernous eyes. Getting lost so quickly in the pull between us. Losing all semblance of how fucked up this situation is and falling into a trance his gaze produces in me.

He flicks a loose strand of hair behind my shoulder, brushing over the bare skin that sends ripples of sensation down to my toes. A flock of birds taking flight in my stomach.

"Trust me when I say, Gemma, that I don't buy innocence," he assures me, his head bent to whisper in my ear. "But I will take it. And before this thing is over, you'll give it to me freely."

It's shocking. I want to deny it. Tell him he's wrong. That there is no way in hell I'd ever hand over my virginity to him, this arrogant asshole of a man holding me against my will.

I open my mouth to refute his claims, to push him away so I have room to breathe, but the words get trapped in my throat when his lips meet the sensitive skin below my ear. My hands flutter wildly before they land on his firm, solid chest. I try to push him away, but instead, grab his sweater to draw him closer.

His warm breath fans out, the scent of minty fresh breath with a tang of bourbon lingering over my neck, the masculine spice of his cologne activating some chemical reaction in my bloodstream.

My eyes close on their own accord, as I tilt my head to the side to offer him more canvas to explore. The sensitive buds of my puckered nipples rub roughly against his shirt as it grazes Faron's chest.

A squeak of excitement escapes my lips when his hand wraps at the base of my neck, drawing me closer, my belly doing crazy acrobatics from the thrill of being handled this way.

I want *more, more, more.*

And he seems to answer the call with the firm press of his hard length between my legs, his foot kicking at my ankle to give him room.

Our bodies are tangled in a dance of possession and need. Desire and control.

Without disengaging his lips from the spot on my neck, Faron walks me backwards in calculated, measured steps until my back is pressed to the wall and Faron's cages me in from the front. His fingers weave through my hair, tugging it into a fist, his fingernails biting into my scalp.

And then his mouth is on mine. The kiss is punishing and cruel, as if a means of transferring all his frustration out on me. His mouth maliciously attacks as his tongue stabs between my lips so that our teeth clank noisily together.

And it is everything I've ever wanted.

It's not the soft peck of my first kiss. Or the grossly sloppy and underrated teenage make-out session with Pete Hanson in the ninth grade.

No, this kiss is powerful, shaking me to the core, rendering me lightheaded as my knees wobble and my heart wickedly thunders in my chest from the roguish manner he masters my mouth. I'm vibrating with need, but as Faron ends the kiss, I realize the vibration I feel against my hip is actually his phone.

Faron backs away so suddenly, I feel as if I'm falling from a dizzying height. He drops his hands from my neck and hair, staring at me with a disassociated scowl. As if he can't quite believe what he's just done with me. Or why.

Everything in me turns cold, shivers manifesting over my skin, skittering down my arms that I cross in front of my chest, hugging my torso tight in a protective gesture.

"Fuck," he curses, his voice roughened by lust, blinking a few times before shaking his head. "What the fuck?"

His question is rhetorical, as he shoves a hand in his pants pocket and removes a phone.

"What?" His answer is brittle and terse, and I wonder if the caller on the other end of the line is surprised by his tone.

There's now three feet between us, but he remains watching me with scrutiny as I try to blend into the shadows as much as I can.

"Roman, I'm busy. What do you want me to do about it?"

I turn my head and notice the mirror on the other wall, seeing my reflection for the first time. My hair is a disheveled mess and my lips are swollen and puffy from the way they were devoured just moments ago. I smooth down my fly-aways as best I can, hoping to regain some semblance of modicum, even though I like my sexy, mussed-up look.

Out of the corner of my eye, Faron edges toward me until he's within inches again. One hand grips the phone to his ear and the other he places at my chin, turning me to face him.

"Yes, I understand. If that's what you want to do, I agree with you. But this has to be sorted out tonight. I have other pressing matters I have to deal with."

His thumb glides over my bottom lip, pressing down at the center so I'm forced to open my mouth. He's so casual about it, looming before me, rubbing the pad of his thumb back and forth. In a bold gesture, I flick my tongue over the smooth edge of his thumb, watching as his dark eyes stoke like black charcoal. And then he shoves it in my mouth forcefully, demanding that I suck.

He narrows his eyes, as if this brings him as much pleasure as it does me. His thumb plunders and explores my mouth, my cheeks hollowing out in suction, electrifying me with bolting currents of lust between my legs.

I'm dizzy with this heady feeling as it courses through me, yet Faron just stares at my lips, his tone flat and unaffected, continuing with his conversation as if nothing is happening.

But his arousal in his pants tell another story entirely.

I grin, circling his thumb with the tip of my tongue, extracting a husky groan from his throat.

"Fine, I'll be there in ten."

And then without warning, his thumb leaves my mouth empty and he turns and walks toward the door. I'm lost in a sea of confusion and lust-filled haze, as conscious thought returns, slowly bubbling back up to the surface.

"Faron?" I ask, my voice sounding brittle and thin.

He breathes harshly but doesn't turn around.

Almost resigned to some decision he didn't make, he says, "I'll send someone up with dinner and an outfit. You're to be ready by nine p.m. sharp. I'll send a driver for you then."

Reeling, I reach a hand behind me, grabbing the wall to keep me steady. It's the only thing that makes sense or has definition at the moment. Everything else just seems foreign, like a French movie without subtitles or dubbing. I'm lost in the beauty of it but understand none of it.

A sharp snap of his head over his shoulder and his gaze locks on me, and a visceral heat forming in the space between us.

"If Mudd won't hold up his end of the bargain, you, Gemma, will be his substitution. And I will get what's owed to me one way or another."

CHAPTER 10

I wait a little over an hour before there's a knock on the door and the arrival of an exotic-looking woman with long silky black hair and a heavy accent.

"Monsieur Blake requested that I attend to your needs and help you get ready. May I enter?"

I gesture her in with a half-smile. She has with her several garment bags and boxes in her arms, another bag slung over her shoulder. Far too much for one petite woman to carry and I immediately offer to help her out.

"Non, non. I'm perfectly fine. Why don't we set up over here?" She points with a chin nod to the desk on the far side of the room. "That will do."

Following blindly behind her, I notice how lithe she is, how elegant. I wonder who she is to Faron. Or Mr. Blake as she referred to him. Is she simply an employee? A family member? Or maybe a lover or girlfriend?

I shake my head free from the ridiculous jealousy slapping me in the face over a man I've only kissed once and who clearly regrets his actions. Or at least, I think he does. Honestly, I can't figure out which way the wind blows with him. One moment he's pissed at me for being associated with my dad, and the next thing I know, he's making grand gestures like this, bringing me fancy clothes and a personal attendant.

As I sit down at her request, she runs her hands over my hair, pulling it back into a pony and out of my face.

"I am Serene, by the way," she says with the eloquent French roll of her R. "First, I will apply your make-up and then we shall do your hair. And finally, we will choose the perfect dress for you to wear tonight for Monsieur Blake."

I blink several times, squinting in confusion as she laughs at my reflection in the mirror.

"Non, non, mademoiselle. We do not want premature lines on this beautiful face of yours." She massages the wrinkles in my forehead with her fingertips, shaking her head as she does.

Her touch and voice are almost hypnotic, as I close my eyes and allow her to work out the stress I've been carrying in my temples and brows.

"Do you know where I'm going tonight?"

I glance at her reflection standing behind me, a tight smile curving at her lips, dark beautiful eyes that catch mine. They express cautious concern.

"Je ne sais pas."

I don't know a lot of French, but I do know that one. She doesn't know where I'm going. Great.

Dropping my chin to my chest, I wring my hands in my lap in frustration until I feel the weight of her hands on my shoulders, drawing my gaze back up and my posture straight.

"There should be no sadness for you. You shall be the most beautiful woman there. I will make sure of that."

I roll my eyes and laugh, but give her a smile, nonetheless. "Good luck with that."

She laughs a dainty, wispy sound. "Nonsense. Vous êtes très belle."

I don't respond but shake my head, as she begins the prep work to get me beautified. This is the first time I've ever had my make-up done and been made to look "pretty." Having always worked hard to downplay any of my feminine features and looks to avoid male attention, it's only now that I have a desire to seek the spotlight from one dark and mysterious man.

Serene continues to work her magic with all the highlighters, brushes, tubes of gloss and powder, and while she does, I sit taller and stare in wonder at the transformation.

"Where in the world did you learn to do this?" I ask in awe, rolling my head side-to-side to seek a different angle.

"I was a model in my teens. Moved from my home country to Paris after my family was killed. But the profession wasn't something I could sustain. And then I met Rome…"

I wait for her to say more, but she busies herself by selecting a sleek black, strappy dress for me, that I slip on and then gush over her genius.

"Wow...just, wow. You do amazing work."

She waves an elegant hand in the air, repacking all the para-phernalia she brought with her.

"Nonsense, darling. When you begin with the perfect canvas, it is simply enhancing the beauty."

I stare at myself in the mirror, running my hands over the sleek lines of the dress, hugging my curves and showing off so much leg it makes me blush.

I'm not the girl that arrived here two days ago.

I'm 100 percent a different woman, ready to prove myself to the world.

But mostly to Faron.

Because the woman standing in the mirror is seductive.

Beautiful.

Powerful.

And she's determined to finish what she came for.

FARON DIDN'T RETURN HOME as he said, and instead I'm whisked away by a car and then ushered into a building with Hulk leading the way, his thick legs eating up the space in the long corridor as I struggle to keep up.

It's a hard thing to do when I've had no practice walking in high heels. I'm clumsy and awkward, growing more irritated by the minute.

"Can you please slow down?" I ask in a breathy voice because I'm nearly winded by the speed in which he's walking.

He doesn't stop or slow down as requested. "No. We have three minutes."

"Three minutes for what?"

He simply grunts and turns a corner, which I obediently do as well. We near a doorway that has two men standing on either side, their dark suits fit nicely over broad shoulders, arms hanging down, crossed in a very militant pose in front of their groins. They appear to be well-dressed bouncers.

I glance at them both as Hulk nods in greeting and unlocks a door with a card. Neither says anything, nor do they move, their arrow-straight backs positioned against the walls in a sentry-like fashion.

The door opens to a bright light ahead, music and hushed voices, and beautiful women dancing on platforms stages centered throughout the room.

It takes a few moments for my eyes to adjust to the darkness as I try to keep up to Hulk like a puppy on a leash. But I get distracted by the women dancing on the platforms.

I think we may be at the same club I was in the first day I arrived, but if it is, it's definitely a different section. From the looks of the men sitting around the room at small cocktail tables, dressed in fine suits, along with the clearly guarded doors, I can only assume this is not open to the general public.

My feet have stopped moving as I watch one woman on one of the stages bend over, presenting her ass and backside as a man takes some sort of whip and hits her with it. I rear back in surprise, my eyes flitting between the two, as he reaches out and rubs a hand over the red mark he just left. Then he grabs her thighs, shoves his head between them and begins licking her pussy as she grinds in his face.

"What *the* -" I mumble in shock before a strong hand clamps down on my wrist and jerks me forward.

Hulk impatiently pulls me along as I stumble behind him, my gaze never leaving the two displaying very intimate PDA. But then my attention is drawn elsewhere as we pass the next platform where a woman is sprawled out on a chaise lounge chair, legs spread wide to hang over each side, her hand between those legs touching herself. Her fingers dipping into her own pussy as she grinds and moans and masturbates in front of the crowd.

My throat is suddenly clogged, parched from both thirst and shock, my mind whirling in alarm as I try to digest what it is I'm witnessing for the first time.

Is this some sort of sex club? Private stripper club? A fantasy-land of kink?

If so, I know I'm way out of my element. This isn't a life I'm familiar with or accustomed to seeing.

A zap of humiliation courses through me, the heat rising like a Phoenix over my neck and face until I'm flushed with embarrassment, mortified over what I'm watching. And, I'm absurdly aroused.

There's no time to analyze my thoughts on the subject matter as Hulk brings us to a screeching halt in front of a table where Faron and two men sit in quiet discussion, seemingly oblivious to what's going on in tantalizing form right in front of them.

Alerted to our presence, Faron stands, whispers something to Hulk who obligingly nods and then leaves me standing there, dazed, confused and very turned on.

A smirk on Faron's face tells me he can read my thoughts. "Like what you see, little girl?"

I huff out a response. "No. It's degrading and disgusting."

He laughs wickedly and winks, reaching around my waist and pulling me close, my hips fitting into his side. "You'll get used to it."

My body tightens as I glare at him, assessing the level of seriousness in his comment, because I don't think I could ever get used to this.

Before I can retort, he pulls out a chair and gestures for me to sit down. I do so reluctantly, feeling trapped under the weight of the two pairs of eyes scrutinizing me from across the table.

Faron makes the introductions. "Gemma, these are my younger brothers and business partners, Roman and Weston Blake."

Even if he hadn't mentioned they were related, it's easy to see the family resemblance in the three men's shared features. While neither of his brothers are quite as dangerously gorgeous as Faron, they both offer attractive traits.

Same dark hair, but variations of the wave and length. Roman's curls around his ears, where Weston's is smooth and slicked back, exposing high cheekbones and an angular jawline. Both are similar in size, with well-defined lean mass hidden underneath their tailored, expensive suits.

As I take in their appearances and features, each one stands and offers me their hands in introduction. Roman's a bit more enthusiastic than Weston, whose hooded gaze gives me chills. As if he has X-ray vision and he's seeing right through me.

"So, you're the jewel thief who fucked us over," Roman muses, sitting back down and crossing a foot over his knee. While he seems relaxed as he sips from his cocktail glass, the words he chooses speaks volumes to the level of distrust, and maybe disgust, he has for me.

The table grows silent under their scrutinizing stares, as I flick a glance to Faron, his eyebrows cocked waiting for me to refute my role in this deal gone haywire.

My voice is shaky, but I square my shoulders in confidence, determined not to let them bulldoze me. It may be three against one, but I've dealt with that my whole life.

"I apologize that my father's actions have created a small hiccup."

Weston, who has been silent, bangs his hand loudly on the table, sending the empty glass skittering and nearly toppling off until Faron intercepts it in his hand. His voice is harsh, cutting like diamond on glass.

"Small hiccup?" He booms, the sound clashing like cymbals even against the noisy backdrop of the club's loud music. "Jesus, lady. That's rich. Because of your father's double-cross, we're at risk now. We have a buyer who has been waiting but is growing very impatient. This is bad for our business."

I swallow my trepidation, which burns like acid in my throat as Roman calmly puts a hand on his brother's shoulder.

"That's enough, West. We'll make this work. Plus, we have her as leverage."

I want to laugh at their belief that holding me for ransom to get my father to play ball will do the trick. He wants nothing to do with me and is probably wondering why he didn't try selling me to the highest bidder long before now.

Because he had other uses for you.

Weston's head snaps to me, a devious glare, his eyes roving over my breasts, to where the material hangs loosely open at my cleavage, which is pushed up seductively in an underwire bra. My hand instinctively rises in modesty to cover myself.

"Taking turns fucking her won't get us what we need," Weston sneers, his lips curling at the corners. Tipping his head to the side, he licks his lips and cocks an eyebrow. "Although, it's been a long time since I've had virgin pussy. It might be a nice change."

"Enough." Faron's stern command has Weston's head whipping toward him, as Faron leans in across the table shaking his finger at his brother in admonishment. "For now, she's off limits to you two, until I say when. Do you understand me?"

At first, I'm relieved to hear how protective Faron is of my virginity and virtue. The kisses we've shared mean something to him, as well. But then realization dawns and understanding comes into view.

Does he mean to share me with his brothers?

CHAPTER 11

Faron orders me some champagne, which I gulp down much too fast, as the three men discuss something about a deal they've brokered that they need to gain entrance into a party in a castle outside of Paris tomorrow night.

I'm paying very little attention, as most of my focus reverts to the stages. I sip my champagne that a waitress brought over, engaging only when I'm pulled into the conversation.

"This is where you are going to make yourself useful to us, Gemma," Faron murmurs in my ear, as I get a whiff of his expensive masculine scent.

My head is filled with bubbles and a lightweight sensation, an intoxication from the champagne and music, the dark, sensual atmosphere of the club, and Faron's own power over me. I seem to go weak at just the sound of his voice, but then mix in his scent and the delicious feel of his fingertips as they glide over my skin on my shoulders, and I'm panting with desire, willing to do whatever they need from me.

All I want is to go someplace where I can be alone with him. To let him do things to me that no other man has ever done. To touch me in the place where I've grown damp and wet and pulsing for him.

A very attractive woman in heels wearing a short, sparkly halter dress stops at our table next to Roman, waving to the men before leaning down and whispering in his ear. The smile that overtakes his face is downright sinful, as he stands, nods to his brothers, and begins to follow the woman down a dark hallway leading to a door where yet another bouncer stands post. I'm intrigued as I watch the movement of his hand as it slides down the woman's bare back and then tugs the back of her skirt up to grab her bare ass.

Faron notices my obvious disbelief, and leans in close, his hand on top of my thigh. "Are you curious about where they're heading off to? And what they're going to do?"

I deny with a shake of my head, but he chuckles a knowing laugh.

Across the table, Weston fishes out his phone from his jacket pocket, looks down to read a message, and then abruptly stands. "I've got to head back down to the Edge to handle a delivery. I'll see you later."

He thumps a hand over Faron's shoulder as he passes and glares at me before he disappears.

Now on my second drink of the night, my tongue and body tingle with a foreign weightlessness, the edges of my reason growing fuzzy and loose. Leaning up to Faron's ear, I ask, "What is this place?"

"A private club."

I scoff. "Obviously. But is it…is it a sex club?"

Faron looks around the room, sweeping his hand wide. "Do you see any sex happening right now?"

I look around at the stages, where women are naked and bare, dancing seductively, touching themselves, and inviting men to touch, as well. The room is full of tables where men watch and drink and talk. But there's no physical sex.

"Well, technically no. But the women…that's not normal to see. That woman over there was getting herself off. In front of everyone." I mouth the words in a loud whisper, which he finds funny.

Faron raises an eyebrow and bellows a laugh, his hand skimming down my arm, grazing the side of my breast just so. "Does that bother you, little girl? Have you never pleasured yourself before?"

I swallow the uneasy lump in my throat, still uncertain why he's brought me here or what he's trying to prove.

"Of course, I have…" I turn my face away, embarrassed to admit this to him.

His finger lodges under my chin as he drags my gaze back to him.

"You've just never seen anyone else masturbate, is that it?"

"God no!"

It's not like I'm completely sheltered or unaware of sexual acts. Growing up, on more occasions than I care to recount, I'd overheard my brother and my dad doing all sorts of loud, sexual things through the paper-thin walls of my bedroom. Sometimes, I knew they'd brought someone home to share their beds, but other times, I could hear the low sounds of whatever porn they were watching and the slick slapping of skin as they got themselves off.

Back then, it made me feel dirty and gross to know what they were doing.

But tonight, I wonder what it would feel like to do that. To be so exposed to a man. To have him watch me with the same lust in his eyes that these men have for these women.

"So, is this club for sex slaves or something?"

I lean into his hand that strokes over my hair, playing with the strands that have dislodged from my updo.

"We do not buy and sell here. Everyone here is eager and willing to share their sexual proclivities with others. They are all here on their own volition."

He pushes back his chair and offers an outstretched hand to me.

"Let me enlighten you, Gemma."

He takes me down the same hallway Roman disappeared into and steps around a black velvet partion. A large ornate door blocks entrance into wherever it leads, and a man stands in a booth in the wall.

"Good evening, sir. It's good to see you tonight, Mr. Blake. It's been awhile."

"Hello Rodney. I'm taking Miss Phillips on back."

"Very well. Has she signed the consent form and NDA? And shall I open a room? Perhaps the Lavender room, sir?"

Both men look at me as I have an answer to the question that I know nothing about.

Faron returns his attention to Rodney. "Perhaps another night. For now, it's simply an introductory tour. I'll have her complete the paperwork at a later time."

"Excellent. Well, have a good evening, Mr. Blake and enjoy yourself. I hope to see you again, Miss Phillips."

The door opens with a mechanical clang, a dark, omniscient noise as we enter. Faron grabs my hand and clasps his fingers through mine. It's dark, save for the red lighting above each doorway and window, which casts a hazy light over the hall-way. Because we're still at the far end, I can't see much of anything from this vantage point. Only a few people milling around the windows.

I choose this moment to ask a question. "Faron, why would I need to sign a consent form?"

He stops and whirls toward me, his head bent down close to my face.

"Gemma, to answer your earlier question, yes, the space we've entered now is a sex club called The Rough Edge. This is a private club, an offshoot of The Edge downstairs, which is public. It has exclusive membership and an exhaustive set of rules that everyone must follow. In order to gain admittance, a person must be invited, and there's only a select few who receive an invitation. Participation is voluntary but requires a non-disclosure agreement and their consent. We don't need sex slaves. We are all, essentially, slaves to sex."

My legs tremble and knees buckle, and I know my face is flushing pink. Because I'm so naïve to this world of underground sex and kink – and for pity's sake, still a virgin - I'm not really sure what everything he's explained to me even means. I step back, my arms dangling at my side, giving myself some breathing room, and dare to look up at him.

He cups my face in his palms. "Let me show you what I want from you, little girl. What I want to do to you if you'll let me. How I want to get off by sharing you in front of others who will watch you get fucked, by me and other men. Do you understand?"

Faron crowds me. Towers over me and uses his body as an effective method to gain my compliance, pressing me back into the door that's now locked shut. The heat from his chest burns through me, yet a chill of the unknown runs down my spine.

My pulse quickens into a rapid gallop, and my nipples pebble and turn into hard diamonds that poke through the lace of the bra and demand attention.

"Gemma, my level of perversion runs deep, and an innocent like you has no idea just what I want to do to you. Want to have you do for me. I want to make you submit, to break you and allow me to use you in the most depraved ways."

Although his words are crude and overtly sexual, and I should be committed because they turn me on, as his thumb strokes gently over my cheek and leaves traces of his warmth behind. It's a soft gesture of desire, not demonized with his lust.

And because of that, I answer truthfully and with absolute certainty.

"Yes, Faron. Show me."

CHAPTER 12

Never even in my wildest and most sensual dreams could I have actually been prepared for what I see. The debauchery and wantonness of what's going on behind each set of windows is in each and every case more tantalizing than the next.

Each room is labeled with a sign above the door, names of various perfumes or fragrances. There is a lavender room. Amber. Vanilla and cinnamon. Clove and jasmine. Sandalwood and bergamot. Rose and ylang-ylang. Faron explains that each of these scents have been known for centuries to trigger electrical neurons in our brains that correspond with our sexual drive and appetite.

"Any preferences?" he inquires, as a door down the hall opens and a woman steps out, naked except for a shawl wrapped around her bare shoulders, as the scent of a spicy amber wafts out. She stops when she sees Faron, lifting her hand with a coy smile and brushing it over the open lapel at her breast.

"It's been awhile, sir," she says, dropping her eyes to the floor, her voice thick with desire and dripping with sex. "Will you be joining us tonight? I'm sure Malik won't mind."

A protective hand wraps around my shoulder as he pulls me into him.

"Not tonight, precious. I have other plans."

The woman's head snaps to me, her eyes narrowing, stinging me with their jealousy. But they are quickly disguised by a mask of phony invitation.

"Your new partner can come watch. I can teach her how to please you, sir."

She's close enough now to reach out and touch me, which she does. Her long, thin finger traces a path along my cheek, softly cooing between her painted lips. Faron swats her arm away, stunning us both at his possessiveness.

"Do not touch what is not offered to you. Now go. I have no use for you tonight."

It's easy to see how offended she is, the hurt flashing in her devious eyes like a bright shooting flare. But it quickly fades as she inclines her head respectfully and whirls around to leave.

The tension in Faron's body is palpable, his shoulders and back strung tight from the interaction with the woman. He offers me no explanation, simply leading me further down the hall toward a window.

Positioning his body behind me, he spins me around in a demonstrative way where my eyes land on a couple inside the room. His grip secures me to him, pinning me there to watch the scene unfold in front of me.

"Watch them."

I inhale a breath as I peer in, the room relatively dark, except for a low light in one of the corners that washes the room in a yellow haze. I blink a few times, adjusting to the darkness, until I see movement.

Toward the opposite wall is a large wooden structure, maybe six foot high. It looks like an X attached to the wall, with leather shackles of some sort on each point. The nearly naked woman is being restrained on the structure, her legs in a spread eagle position, as a man, whose back is to me, wearing a leather mask runs some type of instrument over her exposed breasts and then pulls his wrist back and flicks the end over her very pink and turgid nipples.

I gasp, stepping back into the safety of Faron's broad chest.

"Don't worry, Gem. It's erotic pain. She likes it because it feels extraordinary. It aids in the heightened pleasure of their encounter. The tease of the flog against her sensitive flesh and aroused pussy is soon going to push her into a frenzied orgasm when she's finally given the okay to come."

Faron's hand trails down my arm, slipping over my hip and across my waist until it rests between my legs. A dull ache has been building there since the moment I came here tonight, slowly growing more needy and intense, pulsing furiously in need of touch.

A moan slips out of my mouth as he snickers in my ear. "Does it excite you, little girl? Being a voyeur and watching the sexual appetites being fed and curated right before your eyes?"

He presses his solid length, hard and rigid, firmly into the crevice of my ass.

"You know what turns me on the most?"

I shake my head against his chest, leaning back, rubbing my ass in a suggestive and desperate grind.

"Knowing that this arouses you. Knowing your body responds so greedily to it. Knowing your virgin cunt is dripping wet with the need to be filled."

Everything inside me lights up. Flashes of heat and sparks of lust douse me like fuel, burning through my body like a rocket on its re-entry to Earth.

"Yes," I reply, even though it wasn't a question to be answered, simply the truth. I lift my arms over my head, clinging to his neck, as his hand slinks down the center of my legs, finds the edge of my dress and hikes it up past my hip bones.

"Please, touch me."

His fingers tease circles around the front panel of my panties as I arch into him boldly and wantonly. And then his fingers still, leaving me panting and frantic.

"You will address me as Sir when we're like this going forward," he demands, biting the tip of my earlobe hard, the sharp pain in contrast to the pleasure bubbling up through my blood. "Do you understand me, little girl?"

I nod wildly. "*Y*-yes, sir."

"That's good. Are you still watching them?"

My eyes had been half-lidded from the shameless desire coursing through me, but when I reopen them, I see that the two lovers have been joined by a third player, another man. Upon closer inspection, I realize it's Faron's brother, Roman.

I watch with singular focus, curiosity and a yearning hunger, as Roman drops down to his knees between the woman's spread legs and spreads her lips of her pussy before slowly licking her from back to front, while the man behind him strokes his stiff cock in his hand.

I'm a little shocked to witness this from Roman and a foreign proprietary lust registers inside my head, squeezing my heart with a jealousy I can't pinpoint.

But none of it is as important than the glide of Faron's fingers as they deftly slip inside my panties and into my wet heat.

"Oh Christ, little girl. So wet. So perfect."

My common sense sends cautionary jabs at my brain, reminding me that I am in public and Faron has me half-exposed for anyone to see.

But my sensual desire and the need to be taken by this man wins out. I don't even try to fight it because the only way I will come out of this with my sanity intact is to submit to what he's giving me. To take everything he offers and beg for more.

The slickness of my pussy is everywhere, dripping down my legs as he uses it to open me up, spreading my lips wider, dragging his finger through my juices. His thumb dips inside and then circles my clit as my knees nearly buckle at the relief I feel from his touch.

Faron's other arm launches around my waist to hold me up, but then his fingers thread over my throat with roughened cruelty. He squeezes and I delight in the flex of his hand as my breath stalls in my lungs.

Bolts of arousal barrel through my stomach and down to my toes. Small helpless noises emerge from deep within the caverns of my chest, as I heave ragged breaths.

A powerful finger thrusts inside me, followed by rapid, shallow thrusts that have me seeing stars. I tremble against him, as he makes my body come alive with a need to be filled, the empty space inside me longing for his cock.

Faron continues to ease his fingertips in and out of me and I know they are coated with my desire. He slowly withdraws his fingers, leaving me bereft as he brings a hand to my breast, pushing down the material of the dress and tugging the bra out of the way before he swipes the wetness over my nipple. I nearly collapse, knees buckling, from the intensity of the bolt that erupts like lightning down to my pussy.

And then he paints the same finger over my lips. "Open."

He shoves his fingers over my tongue, and I taste the salty essence of my desire and moan around his finger. Faron then tips his head down, crashing his lips over mine in a harsh, demanding kiss. His tongue lashes over mine, as he rocks against me before pulling away abruptly.

"I fucking knew you'd taste sweet," he growls, his hand returning to my hot, wet seam and continuing where he left off. "I fucking knew it."

Circling, sweeping, thrusting and coaxing. All of it leaves me with no option but to finally let go. As if timed to perfection, the threesome in front of me has switched their positions, removing the woman off the post and laying her on her back-side on a long chaise lounge. Roman is now thrusting his cock inside her spread legs as the other man stands at her side fucking her mouth.

"It's too much…Faron, oh my god."

I don't know if I mean watching the threesome is too much, or the fact that I'm experiencing such intense pleasure that it's too much to bear.

"I know you're close, Gem. This orgasm is mine. Give it to me like a good girl."

"Yes, sir." I whimper.

Faron roars against my ear in appreciation, as my body tenses and bows so tight, I shatter to pieces, breaking apart in a swirling mass of bright lights and explosive detonations.

And then I'm limp, exhausted in a way I've never experienced, as Faron picks me up in his arms and carries me away.

CHAPTER 13

I wake up in my bed alone.

By the way the bright sun streams through the crack in the curtains, I know it must be late morning, but I have no idea what time it is.

Everything comes rushing back from last night when I roll to my side, my body elongating into a stretch, a contented warmth passing over me, like a peaceful brook flowing downstream.

Although as soon as the memory of last night's club experience and the way Faron made me come so explosively, I feel tingles between my legs. My hand moves to cover my mound, fingers poised to curb the ache already building like a volcanic eruption.

Slipping my fingers inside the slick wetness between my folds, I squeeze my thighs together, rubbing over the bundle of nerves that percolate at the mere imagery of Faron's ministrations, his dirty words echoing in my memory that I deliciously devoured and savored as he brought me to orgasm.

A light tap on the door has my breath hitching and my hand flying nervously to my side. Jumping to a sitting position, I reach for the robe on the chair next to the bed and cover myself demurely.

"Mademoiselle, are you awake?" It's Serene, the same woman from yesterday.

"Yes, come in."

Gathering the silk materials over my shoulders, I lift and twist my hair into a bun on top of my head and slip on the slippers left for me so thoughtfully by Serene.

"Monsieur Blake has asked that you join him for breakfast on the terrace. I shall wait for you to get dressed and I will escort you down."

I wave my hand. "It's fine, I can find my own way down."

She gives me a polite, if not tight, smile, tipping her head to the side. "It will be my pleasure. And you are not to be left alone."

Ah, that's right. For all intents and purposes I'm still Faron's prisoner, even if I am treated more like a queen than a captive.

As I run a brush through my hair and freshen up, I decide to use Serene's presence to ask questions about my captor and his accomplices.

"Serene, I met Faron's brothers last night. Do Roman and West live here, as well?"

I stand at the sink, throwing a glance over my shoulder to find her eyes blown wide, her face suddenly flushed with color at the mention of the brothers. Interesting.

She shakes her head, looking down at her feet. "*Non*, Roman and Weston live elsewhere, but are here often. I used to work at the club, for Roman. But he chose to transfer me here."

Her face pales and her voice tapers off softly. I wonder which part of the club she's referring to – the dance club or the ultra-private club. Either way, she doesn't sound like she is happy with the decision.

"What did you do for Roman?"

She smiles, clearly happy to share her role. "He put me in charge of the VIP lounges. I ensured our guests were taken care of properly."

"What happened? It sounds like you enjoyed your job. Why did Roman transfer you?"

I slip out of my pajamas and step into a pair of shorts and a vintage concert T-shirt I'd brought with me, and I follow Serene out of the room and toward the staircase landing. As we hit the top step, she sighs.

"I don't know, exactly. But one night, an important client tried to…well, he made advances on me that…"

She stops, placing a hand clutching her throat, her fingers curling around the banister to hold her up, obviously recalling something painful. I touch her forearm and feel the tremble of her fear.

"You're okay now, Serene. Were you hurt?"

She nods. "I was taken to the hospital. When Roman found out, he was furious. And the next day, I was told I'd be working for Mr. Blake at his home as his personal assistant. And Roman avoids me now. Won't look at me. I think he…"

We take the last step to the landing and I embrace her tightly. There's something about Serene that I connect with. In another life, I know we'd be friends.

"Shh...I think he must care about you an awful lot if he moved you. He's trying to protect you."

As I look over her beautiful ebony skin, her dark hair swept behind her head and plaited in a complex braid flowing down the middle of her back, I now notice a scar that runs along the side of her neck, beginning at her throat where her hand just covered. She sees where my gaze has gone and turns away, shielding it protectively with a hand.

"He is ashamed of my appearance. My imperfection and that is why I no longer work there and can no longer model."

Pushing through a glass door that opens up onto an expansive terrace overlooking a lush private garden below, surrounded by a fortified wall of stone, she offers with a wave for me to enter, as she remains at the door.

"I'll leave you now. Enjoy your breakfast." Serene dips her head, and I catch her eye as we exchange a shared glance.

Faron, Roman and West are all eating breakfast, the table filled with a lavish spread of sweet breads, coffee, fruit and platters of cheese. I notice the way Roman stares off over my shoulder, in the direction Serene has gone. His gaze reflects longing, certainly not shame that Serene believes he harbors.

But then I see Faron, whose stare penetrates me like a hot stoker right from the fire. It burns and sizzles every cell in my body. It eats me up like a wildfire on the rampage.

"We've been waiting for you. There's business to discuss this morning."

His tone is icy cold intonation, lacking any of the passion we shared last night. Now I wonder if it was a figment of my imagination because the warmth has disappeared, like it never even happened.

I take the seat offered to me, saying good morning to everyone. The only one who seems particularly generous in his greeting is Roman, who returns his attention immediately to eating the massive plate of food while West is distracted by his phone.

A member of the house staff pours my coffee, asking if there's anything else I'd prefer to drink, ticking off several fresh squeezed juices to select from. I ask for a peach Bellini and begin to load my plate with a flaky croissant and some fruit.

Faron clears his throat to gain my attention, a serious inflection in his tone that has my nerves on end.

"Gemma, as you know, we've been trying to get in touch with your father to continue our negotiations, but he wasn't returning any of our attempts to reconnect."

I FOLD a napkin over my lap, pinching my brows together as I stare down at my hands.

"Gemma, look at me."

Slowly, I raise my head and see the hard lines of frustration in Faron's inscrutable expression.

"Do you want me to call him?"

Faron's lips purse together tightly, as if whatever he's about to say is bitter.

Weston pipes in. "I don't think that would do much good."

My head snaps to him, a man I don't know at all, but who clearly dislikes me. He's been nothing but rude and contentious toward me since we met.

"Why not? I am his daughter, after all." I say it with conviction, although I'm not convinced of it myself.

West mumbles under his breath. "A daughter he sold…"

"Enough," Faron barks, his demand aimed at West. "Gemma, that won't be necessary at this point. We reached out to our contacts in New York this morning. Your father was found dead. He was shot. I'm sorry."

CHAPTER 14

Everything coming from Faron's mouth is tumbling around my head like a drier of loud static in my ears. A low hum of incoherent noise that doesn't compute or translate and is a jumbled mess.

"Gemma? Did you hear me?"

I'm staring at Faron but don't see him. All I see are faraway memories, flipping through my mind as if on a photo carousel, images moving far too fast for me to even piece-meal them together.

If only everything could just stop for a moment, long enough for me to rid myself of this dizziness and vague disarray. Too many emotions fight for dominance right now - a mix of sorrow, shock, jubilation and disbelief.

My father is dead, and it leaves me vulnerable and unprotected.

"Leave us," Faron says to Roman and West, who immediately do as he commands. They're probably relieved to get out of here and not have to offer condolences to their enemies' daughter.

I take stock of how this news affects me. Should I be a heart-broken mess? Crying in grief? Wailing for the unfairness of it all?

None of those emotions seem to trigger a response. It's as if a wave of calm numbness settles over my body, lifting me from the chains that had kept me prisoner within my father's control since I was born, washing over me with a sense of freedom and gratitude.

Faron crouches on his haunches next to me, tenderness replacing the frozen daggers in his eyes, reaching to place my hand in his. His palm is so large and powerful, yet protective and consoling.

"Are you okay? Do you want to go lie down?"

I shake my head and search my brain for the words to describe what I want and what I need.

"Do they know who killed him?"

His thumb absently strokes the top of my hand. I think about last night and what his hands are capable of doing. How sensual and deliberate they are in coaxing out an orgasm from me. Making me come so beautifully, so unexpectedly.

And now they take on a completely different role, demon-strating a gentle sympathy and calming strength.

Standing, he pulls me to my feet and guides me to his lap as he sits back down in his chair, securing an arm around my waist.

"The police are checking leads, but rumor has it that it may be someone else that he conned. He may have swindled the wrong mark this time."

I flash a hard, questioning look at him, and he shakes his head in denial.

"No, Gemma, it wasn't us. I may have wanted to kill him for fucking with our original agreement but killing him would have done us no good. Now I'm left without a means of getting that diamond and derails my plans immensely. It's possible my buyer might back out entirely, so I need to figure something out fast."

I nod in understanding. "What do you need me to do?"

He gently tucks the hair behind my ear, nipping my earlobe between his teeth.

"Mmm, little girl. That's a loaded question. It pains me not to be able to lay you across this table and take what I need from you this moment." He kisses a strip of skin down my neck, as I delight in the contact.

I pull away. "Why didn't you take me last night? I was willing."

An almost animalistic growl rips from his throat and the hard ridge of his erection grows between us, a physical confirmation he did want to but held back for some reason.

"I could've taken you. You were dripping wet for me, little girl. So wet and eager. I could have made you kneel and had my way with you. Stolen your virginity in front of anyone who wanted to watch me fuck you so hard your voice would've been raw from screaming my name."

I nod, biting down on my lip with a heavy sigh.

"But you didn't. Why not?"

He lifts a shoulder casually. "There will be time. Last night you were under the influence, and I want you completely sober and able to agree to everything with a clear head."

"Yes, I want that."

Scooting from his lap, I drop to my knees in front of him, lifting my eyes to show him the truth and my intentions. Seeing his desire and approval gives me the confidence to proceed.

I run a tentative, shaky hand over his thigh, the soft give of the material so opposite to the rigid swell at his groin.

And this is where I hesitate, because it's all foreign to me. Touching a man, especially an experienced, powerful man, is not something familiar to me.

My voice is a faint whisper. A plea. "Tell me what to do, sir."

We're alone, everyone having left already or back inside the house, but the idea that anyone could peer outside at any moment is a thrilling thought. And based on the atmosphere of the club last night, being watched in front of voyeurs is something Faron enjoys, his proclivity for sexual activities in the open part of his make-up.

He groans, his voice rough and gravely. "I won't be easy on you. I'm going to fuck your mouth hard because you're a dirty little girl. Now take my cock out."

A thrill lights up my spine, tingling with anticipation and yearning. I make quick work of his zipper, undoing the button between my fingers, flipping open the tabs of his pants. The bulge looms large, my mouth salivating to unwrap him in his entirety. To see what awaits me underneath his briefs.

I run my tongue over my lips to moisten them, peeling down the briefs for him to lift his hips as I slowly uncover his cock. My breath hitches as I stare at his length, the way it points proudly upwards toward the sky, begging to be touched.

Faron scoots forward in his seat, legs spread wide allowing me room to square my shoulders and lean in. Breathless with anticipation.

"Open." His fingers wrap around his cock, guiding it to my mouth, which I open for him as I get my first taste of him.

The mushroom tip slides past my lips. Tangy, salty flavor with a hint of masculine musk covers my tongue. I curl my lips around him and suction my mouth, as he surges into the back of my throat.

The tip hits me so forcefully that I gag, my eyes stinging with tears, coughing and trying to catch a breath. My eyes flick to Faron's face looking down on me with an expression of excruciating pleasure. His brows tighten with an edge of restraint.

"That's right, dirty girl. Choke on me. Feel me claiming that pretty mouth of yours. Take me in so deep you'll feel it in your pussy."

His dirty words flood my panties with moisture, my thighs clenching together to ward off the building ache. I slip a hand between my legs with the intent of rubbing my clit to ease the burn, but Faron grabs it with lightning fast speed, capturing it roughly behind my back.

"No touching what's mine to touch. Keep your hands behind your back."

His cock slips from my mouth on a protest, my butt falling back onto my heels.

"But…"

Faron leans forward, bending his head so his face is an inch from mine. "You asked what you could do for *me*, did you not?"

There's no need for me to respond since we both know I said that. The scent of his spicy aftershave is an aphrodisiac like no other, sweetening the abrasive words he utters.

"You will submit to me and do as I say. If you don't, I will punish you. If I'm pleased, then you will be rewarded in return. What will it be, little girl? Do you want to be rewarded?"

I've never wanted anything more. I want to submit to Faron in whatever manner he wishes. I will offer him everything, like a sacrifice, to be his. To be claimed and used and ruined.

Because that's the only outcome. There's no turning back now. I'm a passenger on this train and he's my conductor.

I shift back onto my knees, locking my wrists behind me, and present my open mouth to him once again.

"Good girl."

CHAPTER 15

As a teen girl in Jersey, I never had female friends, nor did I have a mother, which left me very lacking in those all-important heart-to-heart chats about boys, sex and the realities of sexual acts.

Like, for example, how to properly give a blow job.

Perhaps if I'd ever had an opportunity for those private discussions, I would have been more prepared with what to expect when a man comes in a girl's mouth.

As it was, I didn't know.

Once I return to my kneeling position, Faron shoves me full once again as I begin sucking and licking in earnest. Faron's thrusts become faster, wilder and less controlled. I'm overwhelmed with pride knowing that I'm the reason he's losing his carefully managed grip on his restraint.

With one hand holding his cock as he strokes himself in between thrusts to the back of my throat, he weaves his other hand through my hair, cinching my strands between his fingers, tightening it in a fist so hard that my eyes sting and I nearly beg for mercy.

But with every indecent word of praise, he works me through the bite of pain, as I swallow and suck his engorged cock down.

"That's it, little girl. You're so eager…your mouth was made for sucking my cock."

"I bet that virgin cunt is so goddamn tight. And after I take your pussy, I'll claim that ass of yours."

His cock flares and pulsates, carving into my cheek as he says this, the taste of him getting stronger as my saliva coats and lathers him each time he slides in and out.

I ache so badly, my nerves fluttering maniacally like a crazed flock of butterflies, desperate to be touched. I moan my discontent around the head of his dick, the vibration seemingly having an unintended effect on Faron.

Suddenly, his grip tightens, as he surges forward, pumping so deep that once again it chokes me, leaving me gasping for breath as thick ribbons of hot cum run down my throat. I keep swallowing, working my throat against the pressing of his head, as his deliciously dirty words praise me for my very actions.

"Fuck, you're so good. You're taking every drop of my seed like a good little girl. I can't wait to cum inside your sweet little pussy."

Every nerve ending in my body is on fire, painfully pricking at the surface of my skin. When he finally pulls out, the remnants of his release and my own spittle run down my chin. My clit throbs, nipples peaked hard and achey, and my pussy is in dire need of being filled.

While my walls have never clutched a cock inside before, my womb feels depleted and empty, vacantly spasming for his cock to take up residence inside.

For a moment Faron simply lays his head back against the chair, lounging leisurely before fitting his semi-hard cock back into his pants and zipping up. His expression is indiscernible. I slowly rise to my feet, pushing up with my hands on his thighs and shift awkwardly between them, wondering what comes next.

I'm uncertain of the protocol. Will I be dismissed, as he did with that woman at the club last night? Will he return to work, leaving me alone? And more importantly, after the news of my father's murder, am I still considered his captive, or will I be set free?

"You look like you want to say something, Gemma. What is it?"

His tone is effectually back to all business. Had he not been praising me earlier, I might assume my skills in giving head don't meet his standards and leave something to be desired.

But the twitch of his eyebrow tells me he enjoyed everything I did, and I pleased him very much. Which oddly, makes me proud.

Reaching for the Bellini poured earlier for me, I take a drink, the sweet peachy goodness and bubbles mixing flavorfully on my tongue and washing away his essence. I inhale a fortifying breath, noticing how his own breath has already returned to normal.

"What are your plans with me now?"

He lifts the dark eyebrow in a seductive question mark. "I thought I'd made myself clear. I plan to fuck you until your too sore to move."

My mouth forms in the shape of an O, my cheeks pinking in an involuntary blush.

"Besides that," I giggle, waving a hand in the air. "You mentioned you have a job for me to do for you. What is it? And afterwards, am I going home?"

The corners of his lips curve into a seductive smile, the contrast so great between the white of his teeth against the dark stubble over his lips and jawline.

"My eager little girl," he smirks, dragging his thumb over my bottom lip, dipping it into the indentation to open my mouth. "You're going to use this pretty mouth of yours and these exquisitely gifted hands to steal something very valuable for us."

I jerk my head back. "What is it?"

Faron runs his tongue over his teeth. "We'll discuss the details later. In the meantime, I need to handle some business at the shop. I've arranged for a gown to be delivered and Serene will pack you an overnight bag for Paris. I trust you'll have everything you need, but if there's something you'd like, just let her know."

He reaches into his back pocket and pulls out my phone, handing it to me as he stands to leave.

"Feel free to call whoever you need to begin making arrangements for your dad." I grasp the phone between my fingers, but he keeps it secured in his, the action jerking me forward on the balls of my feet, so I fall into his chest. I readjust as he gives me a stern warning.

"JUST REMEMBER, Gemma. Until you fulfill your end of the bargain, you're not free to go. Don't even think about conning me like Mudd did. It would not be in your best interest."

A sudden anger washes over me, a flood of emotion that wells up and churns in my belly. Perhaps it's from the news of my father's death, or the fact that I just did something so intimate with Faron, that his lecture feels like a slap in the face.

In fact, it's riled me up so much, that I can't control myself when I shove him in the chest.

"How dare you? How could you even think that after what we just did. After what I just did."

He lifts an eyebrow, cynicism oozing from his expression and tone.

"Gemma, I don't confuse sex with business. It's best you learn that early, too. Just because you can use your mouth to get me off doesn't mean I'll trust the words of a thief and a con artist."

I huff bitterly and brush past him toward the house, my shoulder bumping his with a harsh, satisfying jolt.

There's a part of me that wants to prove him wrong and make him eat his words, but what good would it do? From the sounds of it, he'll never trust me.

"I may be a thief, but I am not a liar. And I've never broken my promises."

CHAPTER 16

T he train ride to Paris is relatively quiet, the four of us silently contemplating tonight's event and the plans that have been made to extract the intended article.

When Faron had returned from his office, he sat down and explained the objective for tonight and how I would be used in order to achieve the desired outcome.

Since I haven't been able to come through for them with the real diamond, they're putting my useful skills in thievery to good use for their own purposes.

There are documents, apparently very valuable documents, that they need to acquire linking to some stolen property that man named Casper has in his possession. They were very selective in the information they shared with me, however, seeing as they still don't trust me.

And honestly, I was still mad at Faron and chose not to ask questions or inquire any further. I would do as I was told and play the part he needed me to play like an obedient little girl. But I wasn't going to invest myself any more than I had to.

The high-speed train zooms past the landscape that is highlighted only by the light of the moon. Adrenaline spikes through my veins the closer we get to our destination, and maybe some excitement, too.

While Roman and West sit in the First-Class carriage row in front of us, Faron sits next to me in his tux looking very *Mad Men*-esque. I glance down at my attire, the gold silk dress stylishly draping over my body, hugging my waist, and flowing down to my feet that cover my expensive Italian heels.

"Gemma," Faron leans over the armrest between us. I breathe in and inhale the scent of his cologne mixing with the whisky he'd been sipping, my hormones shifting into overdrive. "You look divine. Like a golden goddess. I'm honored to have you at my side tonight."

It's not an apology, per se, but it sure does give me tingles in all the right places. No one has ever complimented me before. I've only been on the receiving end of insults and jabs about my appearance, never looked at as anything but an object.

My big tits made me slutty. My ass sway made me look like a paid prostitute. The bow of my mouth looked like I sucked cock for a living.

Never was there anything positive. So even though they aren't the words, "*I'm sorry*," it's still enough to fill me with hope. A gratitude that Faron takes notice of me and showers me with appreciation and affection.

"Thank you. You look pretty hot yourself tonight, too."

His hand rests on the armrest, palm up, extending it to me in a peace offering. I slip my fingers through his, relishing in the warmth and texture of his protective grip.

Winking mischievously, he tips head to my ear, breath warm and scintillating. "Can I tell you a secret?"

He emphasizes the question with a suctioning kiss on my earlobe, producing delicious and scandalizing goosebumps down my bare arms. He slips the other hand around the side of my neck, cupping the sensitive flesh and drawing me closer to him.

"Mmm-hmm," I purr, delighting in his touch. "I like secrets."

"That night you came into The Edge, and I saw you for the first time - it felt like I was watching a burst of stardust explode across the room. You were so ethereal and glowed so bright. You outshined everyone else around you. I wanted you then and I want you even more so now."

I DIP MY EYES SHYLY, embarrassed to share my own guilty admission about what I thought of him. But he covers his lips with mine, preventing me from saying anything in return. The kiss turns rough and hungry, his tongue plunging into my mouth, exploring me greedily. Bolts of arousal zing through my limbs, my nipples tightening, poking uncomfortably sharp against the material of the sheath dress.

If the conductor walked by right now, he'd likely ask us to get a room, which wouldn't be a bad idea, because just one kiss has my body heating with need. I grow desperate for him quickly, needing more a kiss on my lips. I need his kiss to explore my entire body. For our bodies to collide with such force that the only way we can be any closer is if his engorged cock pushes violently inside me, ripping my virginity to shreds and claiming me as his.

Faron slowly peels himself away, the heat of the kiss lingering on my lips and tongue. His fingertips skim my neck and my jawline before he reluctantly drops his hand onto his lap, inches from the very evident bulge in his trousers. My eyes veer down to his groin and then back to his face.

I'm sure my thoughts are evident across my face, as his reflection in the glass proves it with the slight pull at the corners of his lips. His profile is elegant and handsome but appears conflicted.

"What's the matter?" I ask, pressing my breasts into his side, in search of his warmth and affection. It's like a drug, and now that I've felt the high, I need it often. "Are you worried about tonight? That I won't come through for you?"

He shakes his head, expression guarded but not completely shuttered. "I have no doubt you'll come through."

"Then what is it?"

My nerves take a twisting, looping turn, as fast as this train speeds down the tracks. After tonight, is that it for us? Will I not be of use to him any longer? Will he send me back to Jersey, where I have no real home to go back to?

Fear, panic and sheer loneliness creep inside my thoughts, a fog covering and weighing me down.

"It's nothing for you to worry about. And I'm sorry about my comments earlier. I do trust you, Gemma. And I don't trust easily."

I chuckle sarcastically and flick my chin toward his brothers. "It must be a family trait."

Faron smiles a gorgeous, unfiltered smile that would knock me off my feet if I weren't already sitting down. Normally his smiles are reserved or just downright salacious, but not this one. This smile confirms his genuine love and respect for his brothers. Something I wish I'd had with my brother.

He lifts a shoulder and interlaces our hands together once again. "What can I say? The business we're in has great potential for failure and deceit when we rely on others, as you've seen. Rome and West are the only ones I literally trust with my life and my business."

"I can understand that. I've never had reason to trust anyone, either. Certainly not my father or Johno. They'd turn on me in an instant if it meant protecting their own asses. Bastards."

He squeezes my hand, skimming lightly over the underside of my wrist, the result shooting flames up my arm, hitting me squarely in my heart.

This entire trip and exchange haven't gone according to plan. It was supposed to be an even exchange without any delays or detours. Instead, I've been caught in a dangerous game between two powerful men, been held as leverage, and learned that my father has been murdered. All of it has been complicated and messy.

But tonight, I have the chance to prove to Faron and the Blake brothers that I can turn this thing around and become a valuable asset by proving my worth. I'll successfully fulfill my end of the bargain by stealing from Casper what they want, eliminating my virginity as the only bargaining chip for my freedom.

And then I'm free to give it to whomever I choose.

CHAPTER 17

The party is a lavish scene, with beautiful people all speaking in foreign languages that I don't understand, as they eat, drink and revel in the most luxurious residence I've ever seen before. They certainly don't have this sort of antique opulence where I live. The Soprano's house in Jersey's got nothing on this medieval castle.

As the four of us enter into the home, we're patted down and scanned at the door by security. I can feel beads of sweat roll down my back, while one look at Faron shows that this doesn't faze him one iota.

Roman and West head off to the bar to get drinks as Faron and I casually mingle and work the room. Once I've located the mark, the plan is to create a diversion so I can extract what's needed to complete the plan.

In essence, I'm using not only my pick-pocketing skills to pull this off, but also my feminine wiles.

We make our way through the crowded interior, expensive paintings lining the walls and imported champagne flowing,

Faron quietly pointing out my mark for the night. Casper Foquette, which he pronounces with a French roll of the tongue, *fokay*, is an importer of high-quality merchandise. Although Faron was elusive in describing the product that we would be stealing from him.

My job is to get close to Casper in any manner that I deem fit, which by my estimation will require some flirting, drinking and playing the drunk bombshell. All the while isolating a key card that will be used by the brothers to break into a locked room.

Roman returns from the bar with two drinks, handing them to the both of us as his eyes make contact with mine.

"You got this Gemma?" He seems apprehensive and clearly worried about my capabilities.

Proving myself is essential right now. I need them to believe in me.

I take a sip of champagne, the bubbly essence tickling my tongue and throat as the sweetness floods my mouth with flavor. I step into Roman's space, and his brows skyrocket with surprise, flicking to Faron with question. I lift to my tiptoes, pushing my breasts into his chest, his body ram-rod stiff with tension. Wrapping my arms around his waist, I seductively slide my hand down his spine and lower back and brush my lips to his ear.

"I've got this, Rome. Everything will go as planned on my end. Your end is another story."

I emphasize this with a playful squeeze of his ass cheek, as he jolts from the unexpected physical contact.

After what I saw the other night at the club, and seeing how effortlessly gorgeous and charming Roman is, I have no doubt that he is on the receiving end of female attention all the time. But it does wonders for my confidence to see a flush run over his neck and his breathing accelerated and stuttered as I step back next to Faron.

With a smug grin curving at my lips, I turn to Faron and hand him Roman's phone that I just swiped out of Roman's pocket, lifting my eyebrows in challenge while taking another sip of my champagne. Laughter erupts from Faron's chest as Roman blindly feels around his pants, disbelief registering in his expression, as if he can't believe he was just hoodwinked by me.

Faron hands the phone back to Rome, shaking his head in laughter at his brother. "I believe this is yours, Doubting Thomas."

Turning to me, he brushes his lips over mine and before I can get lost in the kiss, he pulls back, raising his glass in a toast. The glasses clink and sparkle, the sound signifying a brilliant night ahead.

"Drink up, Gem. We've got work to do. The sooner we conduct business, the sooner you and I can get down to our business."

Roman rolls his eyes, tipping back the glass and finishing his drink in one large gulp. When his gaze returns to me, there's a streak of envy, but it disappears just as soon as he wishes me *bon chance* and then turns to return to the bar. We watch him return next to West, who is chatting with a tall, model-thin woman, and I wonder if one or both them will end up sleeping with her tonight.

"You ready, little girl?" Faron asks and I note the double-entendre laced within the statement.

Because while the job I'm here to do tonight is not without some danger, and there is the element of risk ratcheting up my excitement, it's nothing compared to the level of excitement for what's to come afterwards.

When Faron will reward me for a job well done.

And I'll give him a piece of myself I've saved all this time just for him.

"Oh, my goodness, I am such a clumsy mess. Look at what I've done!"

The drink I accidentally spill on Casper's tux coat drips down his lapel, as his face turns from an angry scowl to sly wolf the moment he turns to see who bumped him. I'd been walking by as he spoke to a party guest, and lost my balance, flinging my drink in his direction.

I awkwardly sway on my heels, looking like I'm about to do a face plant, and catch his arm in my death grip. He takes the bait, gallantly reaching to save me and throws a hand around my waist. I giggle for good measure.

"There now, honey. You just had a little misstep. No harm, no foul. No sense for a beautiful woman like yourself to cry over spilt milk."

Casper clicks his tongue, his hand squeezing my side, scaling my waist until it's planted right underneath my right breast. How convenient of him.

"But it's such a waste of good champagne. Whoever the host is tonight, they did such a perfect job organizing such a beautiful party. The food was exquisite and the beverages, ooh la la. I may have had a few too many. But I wish I could properly thank the host for such a lovely party. I'm having so much fun."

I let my knee buckle, my body collapsing into him, my chest now smashed up against his torso and groin. He grows thick and hard underneath, and it takes everything in me not to gag.

"Well, you are a lucky girl, Mademoiselle..." He's looking for my name.

"Madeleine," I respond wide-eyed with a breathy smile. "Like the little shell cakes."

Casper rumbles with laughter, as if that's the funniest thing he's ever heard.

"Ah, what do you know. Those are my favorite French pastries. I can't get enough of eating Madeleines. So petite and deliciously sweet and moist." He licks his chops obnoxiously, so obviously proud of his crude comment cleverly disguised as an innocent remark.

I have him right where I want him.

At this point, the two men he'd been talking to have wandered off, leaving Casper's undivided attention on me. I smile up at him biting down on my lip like an ingenue, my hands touching and caressing his torso as if I'm so enamored with him, I can't help myself.

But instead, I'm search of his wallet and key card.

"And who are you? Do you know the host?"

116

He chuckles. "Casper Foquette. Your drenched party host at your service."

My hand runs over his front lapel, the dampness from the champagne already seeping in, as I skim down the front and near his pants pocket. I cringe inwardly as my hand brushes over his erection but find what I'm looking for despite the interfering appendage.

I peer up into his eyes, flashing demure baby-doll blues. "Casper, I'm the world's worst guest. I really soaked you with my drink. Can I get something to clean you up?"

His response is the darkening of his eyes, and a grin that spells out his love for sex with young women.

"Maybe you are right, Madeleine. Perhaps I should go clean up. Would you like to help me? Somewhere more private?"

Bingo.

This couldn't have worked out more perfectly. I give the signal to Faron, who stands on the opposite side of the room, who then motions to Rome and West from their positions.

With the switch of my purse from one shoulder to the next, I've signaled to them all that I have the card in my possession and the fun can begin.

Sliding my arm inside Casper's tucked elbow, he escorts me through the crowded room, nodding his head to partiers and guests, all while his other arm is slung low around my waist and he gropes my ass.

Just as we near the bar area, heading toward what I presume to be his personal living quarters, Faron comes in hot, approaching me with the scariest scowl I've ever seen, his jealous rage almost a real entity.

"Where the fuck do you think you're going with my girl, Foquette?" Faron shouts loud enough to cause everyone in the vicinity to stop talking and turn toward the interruption.

Faron grabs my hand forcibly, jerking me from Casper's hold, and I smoothly and covertly slip the card into his palm.

And that is teamwork.

"You lying, cheating whore. You were going to fuck him, weren't you? Had I not shown up, you would've slept with him."

All eyes are on us, as Casper stares appallingly between Faron and me, wondering what the hell is going on.

"Mr. Blake, I think you've misinterpreted what's going on between Madeleine and myself."

"Shut the fuck up, Foquette," Faron growls, pushing Casper with a palm against his chest, sending him reeling backwards.

As if he's one of those inflatable advertisement signs used in front of car washes and oil change places, Casper reestablishes his balance and puffs out his chest like he's about to beat on it Tarzan style, ready to stake his claim.

He wrenches my arm back from Faron's grip and stands with a protective hand in front of me shielding me from Faron who steps into a fighter stance, aggressively pressing his nose right into Casper's face.

"I will not have you speaking to this woman in such a disrespectful manner. I do not need for any lover's quarrel to be aired publicly in the midst of my own party. I think the lady should decide what she'd like to do."

We are now the center of attraction with all eyes on us, leaving it wide open for Rome and West to collect the access card from Faron, as they step up behind him, under the guise of rubbernecking with the rest of the crowd, and make the transfer.

From there, the tactical part of our plan is in full swing, as Faron continues to escalate with the name calling and yelling, until finally Casper realizes he can't handle our lovers quarrel and Faron's belligerent outburst.

He calls in for reinforcements, which is exactly what we'd hoped he would do.

With the three security guards removed from their posts and the entire party focusing their attention on what's happening in the center ring, Rome and West are free to blend into the crowd and make their way into Casper's private quarters, where they will gain access and steal what they came for.

Big Head #1 and Big Head #2 surround us, but not before Casper offers me a chivalrous alternative.

"Madeleine, I think we could still salvage this evening if you'd like to stay here with me. Otherwise, you're free to go with this monster and never return here again."

As Faron is dragged out of the party by the two gigantic bodyguards, I clutch my purse and act as if I'm giving his offer some serious consideration.

"Thank you, Monsieur Foquette. I deeply regret the trouble we've caused." I place an apologetic hand on his arm, a rueful smile to demonstrate my sincerity. "But I'm afraid I must go."

I step onto my tiptoes and place a chaste kiss on Casper's cheek, noticing the heavy scents of whisky, sweat and a strong aftershave. Nothing like Faron's intoxicating scent.

"Bon nuit, Madeleine. Another time then. Be safe."

Speaking of safe, as I walk away toward the front entrance, out of the corner of my eye I notice Rome and West have already returned and are having a drink at the bar. An indication they got what they came for without problem or interference.

Our job here is done for the night and I'm filled with a feeling of pride for having contributed to their scheme. Even a small part of it.

And now I'm looking forward to the rest of the night's celebration.

CHAPTER 18

Faron waits for me in the Uber he ordered, his phone lighting up in his palm as I open the door and slide in next to him. His devastating smile unlocks something inside my heart that has never been opened before.

Love. I've fallen in love this man.

The minute the car begins to move, Faron is on me, his mouth crashing against mine, lips tasting and devouring me, his fingers stroking my cheeks in a velvety caress.

His deep voice cutting through the silence as he breaks our kiss. "You were perfect, Gem. Absolutely perfect."

I suck in a breath, acknowledging that the hard part is now over, and we accomplished what we came to do. The knowledge of what comes next ignites and stirs my blood and body. I want Faron in a desperation so deep it penetrates my soul.

"Thank you," I whisper breathlessly. "Are we meeting up with Rome and West tonight?"

What I'm not explicitly saying is whether Faron has plans to fuck me now or later. Because the rush of adrenaline and excitement swirling in me is a fire that needs to be extinguished and contained. ASAP.

And the only way I see that happening is if Faron makes good on his promise.

His intimate grin, laced with sex and powerful lust, tells me we're on the same page.

"We won't see them again while we're in Paris. This weekend you're mine."

The rest of the car ride is a blur of dirty talk and kisses that inflame me so hot, I'm surprised the seats don't set fire. Faron's hands explore my body, touching and kissing, his tongue trailing erotic paths down my delicate, sensitive flesh, red hot surges of lust ricocheting like bullets hitting their targets. Every once in a while, I notice the Uber driver's gaze flicking to us in the rearview mirror and his throat clearing, but he says nothing.

My panties dampen, wet with desire, and I squirm anxiously against the seat seeking friction to the dull the ache and sensation formed there.

"Be patient, little girl. I'll fuck that pain away soon enough. Your sweet cherry pussy will take everything I give you and you'll cry out for more."

I murmur a resounding yes. "Yes, please."

The car comes to an abrupt stop in front of a building along a busy and vibrant street. Having not paid any attention to where we were going, I step out of the car in a daze, briefly scanning the block up and down the street.

There are shops and sidewalk cafés, one in particular with a grand floral arbor above the café door. Across the street is a small cathedral, built in the similar Gothic style as I saw in Antwerp - it's massive pillars and doorways works of art that I imagine took years to build and an artist design.

"Where are we?" I ask in awe, turning in a circle to take it all in.

Faron's hand nestles in the small of my back, stopping my circling and guiding me toward the entry of the building. There's a massive wood-carved door painted a bright blue, with an ornate circular knob in the middle of the door.

"We are in Saint-Germain-des-Prés, the 6th arrondissement of Paris."

I nod as if I know what that means. "What is that church behind us?"

"That's the oldest cathedral in Paris, Abbey of Saint-Germain-des-Prés. Just down the street a few blocks is the River Seine."

The door opens with a *snicking* sound returning my attention to Faron, and he swings the door open to reveal a beautiful, ivy covered courtyard. Holding it open for me to pass, he chuckles as I hesitantly step through to the other side.

"Perhaps you'd prefer we tour the City of Light?" He whispers in my ear, his tone amused and teasing. "Instead of coming up to my bedroom, where I plan to show you a different version of light?"

My head whips around and I press my palms to his chest.

"Faron, Paris can wait. I'm ready to be with you tonight...to give you..." I can't quite say the words, the blush blazing up my cheeks. Can't express how deeply I want to give him everything.

At least my father did one thing right before he died. It wasn't his intent, but he gave me a gift when he sent me to Faron.

The door closes behind me, leaving us protected in a court-yard filled with ivy and botanicals, the scent of orchids thick in the air.

My mind goes blank as his lips take possession of mine, his hands clasping around my neck holding me to him so he can take his fill, kissing a line down to my throat where he sucks and licks, a tiny sound escaping my lips. I swing my arms around his neck, clinging to him, pulling him closer.

"Good girl."

With a swift swirl of his hands, he lifts me off my feet with his hands on my ass, my legs instinctively wrapping around his waist as he carries me through an arched interior doorway and down a hallway where he stops at the entrance to a bedroom.

The room illuminates with a soft glow when he flips the switch, my eyes roaming over the furnishings and layout.

"You will get undressed, leaving your panties on, and kneel at the foot of the bed with your hands behind your back."

"But..."

An argumentative response is about to leave my tongue, a disobedient reply, only for the fact that I want him to undress me. I want to feel his hands touching every part of

my body, to strip me from my old life and give me new
purpose.

I open my mouth, but his narrowed eyes brook no argument.

"In here, little girl, you obey. Otherwise, there will be consequences."

Slipping his bow tie free from his collar, he licks his lips,
slowly roaming down my body and back up again in a
sensual motion.

"In fact, I think I will demonstrate what your sassy mouth
gets you." He spins his finger in the air. "Turn around."

His commanding order sends a thrum of excitement beating
wildly between my legs, the moisture pooling, my breasts
tingling with heaviness. I can't help but rub my thighs
together to alleviate the throb.

"Kneel, bend over the bed and lift your dress. Present your
ass to me."

I turn around and grab at the silky material, lifting it with
both hands to bunch at my waist, the cool air hitting my legs
and ass as a reminder of how exposed I am. With elbows
pressed into the duvet cover, I bend my torso over and lean
into the mattress, sinking into its gentle give, my knees
digging into the plush flooring.

Keeping my face buried into the bed, I wait, wondering what
Faron is going to do to me. The only sound I hear is the
removal of his shoes and belt, the thud and metal clank
echoing in the room.

Suddenly, his index finger is there, trailing over the scalloped
edge of my thong, caressing back and forth before it runs

down the crease of my ass. With a pinch of his finger and thumb, he pulls the satin string from its resting place and slowly slides his finger through the crevice, down, down down, until he reaches my wetness.

My breath stops, and I manage to suck in tiny sips of air, the anticipation so great it nearly suffocates me.

His finger dips into my wetness and drags it over my clit. A sensation so great it ripples like a wave through my entire body as I shudder and moan. I turn my head to the right, resting my cheek over the soft down of the comforter, my lips parting on a pant.

"I'm going to fucking ruin this virgin pussy with my cock, little girl. The same cock you sucked on and fucked with your mouth. I will take great pleasure in coming inside this sweet, tight cunt."

His finger flutters at my entrance and my hips undulate on their own accord.

"Please…"

Smack.

The viciously quick bite of his hand is harsh and victorious all at once, leaving a sting of flesh against my ass cheek.

"Mmm," I moan, because the sting quickly transfers a new sensation zapping straight to my clit.

Smack. Smack. Smack.

The sound is a resounding crack as he spanks me in measured succession.

And then he hums a low, vibrating growl. "This ass…this perfect ass…"

His words seem to dissipate into the air, as he washes away the pain with a gentle caress of his hand, soothing over the flesh that throbs like a million tiny pinpricks under the skin.

I hear his shaky breath as he backs up a few paces, the sound of his zipper unzipping loud in the silence, as his pants drop to the floor in a whoosh. I watch him in my peripheral, my face pressed into the bed.

He kneels behind me, as if this is all too much to remain standing. With both hands, he palms my ass cheeks, lifts me off my knees and pushes me up on the bed. I fall forward with a thump, throwing a hand over my head to keep from going ass over tea kettle. But I guess that's the purpose, as his fingers dig in and he spreads me wide.

Oh my God.

"So pink and pure," he groans, his nose right there in the middle of my most private place. And then he inhales a long hungry breath, groaning wildly.

With a quick snap, the floss of my thong is gone, his tongue replacing it. The tip of his tongue traces a path from my clit to my entrance, the slick sound the most erotic thing I've ever heard.

"Holy shit…" I squeak, uncertain if I should be embarrassed by how turned on this makes me.

Shamelessly, I grind my hips into the bed, whispering a plea for a cure for the ache that's mounting inside me. Faron is my remedy, and the only thing that will make me feel complete.

He flattens his tongue and samples me again, spearing me over and over with his swirling tip. Noises of pleasure escape through my parted lips, mimicking the ones from his mouth, each time escalating louder and louder.

Faron is fucking me with his tongue like a man possessed. A starving man who feasts on my body, like it's his personal banquet of flesh and bone.

He hisses a curse, a ragged mixture of frustration and need, replacing his tongue with a finger, breaching my pussy entrance and slamming it in deep. No hesitation, no warning. Just hard and penetrating. So hard my upper body lurches forward on the bed, the arm above my head holding firm and steady as he fucks me with a punishing finger.

"You like it hard and unforgiving, don't you, little girl?"

I rock my hips back, seeking friction and in search of that elusive orgasm that hovers out in the distance. So close I can almost taste it.

The need begins to spiral inside me, twisting and turning, like a corkscrew pulling out the cork – turn by turn. Each push and flick and drag of his finger loosens me up, my inner walls quivering in response.

Until…until a torrent of sensation rips through my limbs, centering low in the base of my spine and clamors to escape. Like the pressure in a carbonated bottle, my orgasm shakes me until I'm detonating into a million pieces, everything in me spasming and tightening and exploding in a chaos of light behind my eyes.

He promised to show me the City of Light. I just had no idea it would be right behind my eyelids.

I grab at the bedding in my fist, shoving it in my mouth and biting down to muffle the deep keening sound that I never knew existed inside me before this moment.

"*Ahhhh...*" The cry escapes my lips, as his fingers crook inside, the angle adjusting just so to hit that ever-elusive button that sends me skyrocketing to greater heights.

"Oh God. I'm coming...*again*...oh, God..."

The seismic shudders that rack my body have left me depleted, barely able to lift my head to watch Faron behind me. I close my eyes, grateful for the reprieve as he withdraws his fingers, now coated with my essence, and flips me over, grabbing at my heels and yanking my legs open.

When I peel open my heavy lids, he stands over me at the end of the bed, naked from the waist down, his shirt still on, hard shaft in his hand, leisurely stroking himself with my wetness lubricating his cock.

His eyes flare with something stronger than desire. "You are the perfect image of prom virgin and sexy little slut with your gown all rucked up and your pink cunt glistening with your arousal."

Faron moves between my legs, taking my wrists in hand and stretching them above my head, pinning my body beneath him. I peer down between us, as he slides over me, his cock brushing through my wet folds.

Oh, it feels so good.

So, so good as the hard length of him rubs over my clit. My inner walls clench and contract, a profound emptiness that only he can fill.

I experiment with a pump of my hips. "Please, Faron. Just do it. I need it…"

He stops, his eyes narrowing on me. "Please, what?"

Shifting on top of me, his cock hits squarely over my sensitive nub so that I can barely manage a breath.

"Please…sir," I grunt.

"Good girl. Once I'm inside you, I won't hold back. I'm going to fuck you until my seed is dripping from your pussy and you'll feel me for days to come."

For a second I'm still stuck on the image of him coming inside me and what it will feel like as his hard cock rips me apart.

He nudges my legs wider, guiding the tip of his cock to my entrance where it slips in an inch, enough where I can feel the stretch.

"Now I'm going to claim what's mine."

And he shoves his way inside, taking my most valuable possession.

The one I've freely given.

CHAPTER 19

P ain. Yes, there's pain.

But it's just a pinch, and once I've adjusted to the intrusion inside my body, I begin to relax, as he whispers words of praise and adoration.

"Fuck, little girl. Your cunt is so tight. So perfect."

Faron presses his face into my neck, the deep rumble of his voice so delicious that if it had a taste it would be melted caramel.

"Are you all right?"

His body hovers over mine, still as a statue, the place we're joined still a dull ache, reduced from the first biting sting. I wiggle a little under him, wishing I had my hands free to touch his body. To slip my hands under his shirt and score my fingernails down the taut ropey muscles of his back and dig into the perfect flesh of his ass.

"I'm fine. It's okay."

He hums his approval. "My good girl. So, fucking sexy and willing. I can't wait to fuck you at the club. For everyone to see for themselves how precious this tight pussy is."

I gasp, my breasts heaving at the thought of being on display for not just Faron, but for anyone to watch.

And then I remember what he'd promised to do. He'd told me he was going to deflower me at the club. But here we are, in the privacy of his Paris flat.

"Why didn't you wait to fuck me there?"

He withdraws, holding himself still above me, eyes blazing heat and lust and fire. I dip my gaze to his cock that throbs between us thick and long, shining with its tight skin and the wetness from my pussy.

And then he flips me over onto my stomach, pulling me up to my hands and knees and adjusting the skirt over my bottom. His hand smooths over the round of my butt before giving it a deafening smack.

"Are you questioning my decision, little girl?"

"N-no, sir."

"Good. Now lean down on your elbows."

I do as he says, the posture making me feel exposed and vulnerable. I hear the distinct sound of him sucking and spitting, and then I feel the wet tip of his finger circle my anus and I tense up.

"Mmm. Maybe I selfishly wanted this virgin pussy all to myself this time. But I'm more than willing to share this virgin ass with an audience. Would you like that?"

He uses his thumb now to dip inside the tight bud, to open it up, the sensitive nerve endings singing an odd chorus of pain and pleasure. Of forbidden desire and kink.

"I-I don't know, sir. I might be nervous."

His groan is punctuated by a stab of his cock back into my wetness, sinking in so much deeper in this position. I cry out from the invasion, but as he thrusts in and out in a seductive tempo, pain giving over to the pleasure. He grabs a handful of my hair in his fist, tugging it back from my scalp so my head tips back and then turns to the side.

Faron leans over, capturing my lips with his in a deep, lustful kiss. His tongue roams my mouth, his moans mix with mine, as his legs slap against my ass. When he ends the kiss, I drop my head between my shoulders, gasping air and fighting for breath.

His thrusts become more aggressive, more rapid and with every press of his pelvis into my hips, I feel his cock hitting something deep inside me. My own shouts of ecstasy denote the spot he continues to hit each and every time his hips drive into me.

"Faron," I cry out, unable to articulate anything else.

"That's right, Gem. I'm the one fucking you. No one else. I'm claiming this pussy as mine."

I feel something intense clawing at the base of my spine, winding its way through my belly and reaching deep, deep inside me.

"I feel your cunt clamping around my cock. Fuck, it feels so good. You're going to come again, aren't you, my filthy, dirty girl? You're going to come on my cock like a good fucking girl."

He pumps and pumps, and then reaches around the front of my legs, the hair on his arm tickling my stomach, as his fingers deftly find my clit.

And just like that, I scream out my climax, as he bellows out his own release.

His grip on my hips loosens as he pulls out, leaving the sticky residue of his release dripping between my legs. I'm not sure how to clean myself up, so I gingerly roll over to the side of the bed and get up.

Faron watches me through his dark hooded eyes, his body lying limp across the bed, his head turned to the side as he watches me go.

"There's towels in the cabinet you can use if you need a shower."

"Okay, thanks," I reply meekly, flipping on the bright lights of the bathroom.

Closing the bathroom door behind me, I hold the dress in my hands and stare down between my legs.

Blood mixed with semen stains the insides of my thighs, the remnants of my virginity and innocence. Tears well up in my eyes, unbidden, for the loss of something I cherished. I sit down on the commode and softly cry, confused over the sudden emotion sweeping through me.

I finish using the toilet and wash my hands under a warm stream of water, eying the big bathtub in the corner of the bathroom. I grab a towel and stand at the edge of the platform bath, ready to bend over to turn on the hot water when a knock sounds at the door.

Faron opens it a crack. "Gem, can I come in? I should've asked if you were alright."

"Yes, of course." I sniff, trying to rein in my emotions.

He steps up behind me, turning me to face him, scanning over my face that I'm sure is red and puffy from tears.

"Hey, are you crying?"

I wave a hand in the air. "It's nothing. I'm just being a stupid girl."

"Come here," he shakes his head, fingers lacing through my hair. "You're not at all. Until I saw the blood stains, I was so completely lost in you that I forgot. I'm not used to being tender with my lovers. I haven't taken someone's virginity since…"

He chuckles to himself. "Well, it's been a good fifteen years. And I sure as hell didn't handle it well back then. So maybe this is a chance to redeem myself."

Faron kisses my cheeks, each kiss wiping away the tears left behind.

"Thank you," I sigh.

"Let me draw you a bath. Let me take care of you, Gemma."

CHAPTER 20

N o one has ever taken care of me like this. The
gentle caresses and the sweet words he says as he
turns the faucet on, filling the tub with hot water,
steam creating a warm cocoon of silence around us.

Faron sits on the edge of the tub, his hands on the zipper of
my dress, as he slowly undresses me, unfolding the material
over my curves and down to the floor. I cross my arms over
my breasts, feeling oddly insecure standing naked in front of
him in the bright florescent light.

His caress is so gentle, like a feather fluttering over my skin,
just a hint of touch.

"Don't be shy. Let me see how beautiful you are."

He clasps my wrists and unfolds my arms, the warmth in his
eyes drinking me in, worshipping me in his gaze, as he
swings my legs up into his arms and places me carefully and
with ease into the awaiting tub.

I sigh, moaning into the luxurious heat seeping into my sore and aching muscles.

"Are you joining me?" I offer in invitation, scooting into the middle of the large oval-shaped tub, drawing my knees up to my chin.

"There's nothing I'd like more."

Faron climbs in behind me, settling me against his chest, his fingers lightly stroking down the curve of my neck and arms. The feeling is incomparable, and it fills me with a warm contentment that unlocks something inside my heart.

I DISMISS the thought quickly with a mental shake of my head. Even if I love him, I can't stay here with Faron. I've been working on my freedom, and now that my father is gone, and with Johnno still in jail, I'm free to leave. I've done what was expected of me, and now I have to go.

I can't be caught up in a love affair with a man like Faron. He's too worldly. Too dominating. Too powerful.

But you like that.

The deep rasp of his voice interrupts my internal dialogue.

"What's going on in this pretty head of yours?"

I bite my lip, still puffy and swollen from his kisses, and debate whether I should open up.

"I was just wondering what happens now? I don't know what I'll do from here. All I've ever known is life with my father."

A strand of hair falls into my eye and I try to bat it away, but Faron tucks it behind my ear, kissing it in place.

"I suppose you first need to get his house in order. Did he have a will in place?"

I lift a shoulder and give a harsh snort. "Doubtful. And if he did, everything would likely be left to my incarcerated asshole of a brother."

Shifting to the right, I turn my head to the side to look at him. "I don't have the same type of relationship with Johno that you have with your brothers. My brother despises me and would much rather see me dead then ever treat me like a sister should be."

My memories of my childhood are nothing short of miserable. I can't think of a time when Johno had ever looked out for me or stood up and protected me like an older brother should. He was a bully then, and he's a criminal now.

Faron seems to ponder this before asking, "When is Johno's release date?"

I try to remember what he was sentenced for and his anticipated release schedule. "He's coming up on three years, I think. Why?"

Burying his face in my neck, he plants kisses along the curve, as I tip my head away to give him freedom to explore.

"Because I don't want him anywhere near you when he gets out. Do you believe he's in on Mudd's scheme and knows where the diamond is?"

I consider the possibility. It wouldn't be unheard of for Mudd to include my brother in on the plans, as some kind of sounding board or play keeper.

Just then, an idea bursts through my foggy, steam-bath brain, and I jolt up and shift my butt around, my legs sloshing the water nearly over the edge.

"What if…what if Johno is in on it? What if he knows where the jewel is? Maybe I can go home and try and find it. And if I can't, I'll figure out a way to get Johno to tell me where it is."

Skimming his fingertips over my legs, he grabs my criss-crossed heels and pulls me forward, wrapping them around his waist so our bodies connect, his length arching between us, and my eyes grow wide, but he ignores it for the moment.

Smoothing my hair on my head, he cups my cheeks tenderly.

"That doesn't sound safe for you to go alone. I don't trust your family, and with your father out of the picture, I think Johno has a lot on the line right now, even if he's still in prison. Either I'll come with you or I'll send Dempsey with you."

My eyebrows quirk up. "Dempsey?"

He lifts a shoulder, kissing my nose. "You call him Hulk."

I chuckle and let my eyes drift down between us, my cheeks flushing from the water temperature and the protectiveness in his decision.

In just the short time I've known him, Faron makes me feel cherished and valued. And it means everything.

Sinking my hand under the water line, I reach for his engorged cock, wrapping my fist tightly around it with a tight squeeze. Faron smirks, his eyebrow lifts, but a groan escapes between his sexy lips.

"Just what do you think you're up to, little girl?" he questions, slipping his hand behind my back and lowering it over my ass. Cupping my cheeks, he lifts me onto his thighs so the head of his cock nestles at my entrance.

My head falls back onto my shoulders, as Faron leans in and swirls a tongue over my nipple. It's a lightning bolt of sensation, zapping straight down to my toes and has me squirming on his lap.

His lips descend over my breast, covering it with wet, open-mouth kisses in between bites and suckling, leaving marks that flame red and hot. He tests the firmness of my breast in one hand, plumping and squeezing the heavy flesh, capturing the hard bud between his teeth.

I let out a shriek, which lodges his dick more firmly at my opening, but he doesn't push in, even though I wiggle and gyrate wantonly.

"You'll be sore, Gem."

Yes, very possibly. But I'd rather have that brief sting of discomfort then the torment of not feeling him inside me again tonight.

I glide myself over his protruding cock, water sloshing around us, moaning when his ridged tip rolls over my clit. I pull myself up with my hands on his shoulders and sink down onto him, pinching my lips together and breathing in through my nose as I work through the ache.

Finally, when he's seated all the way, and the pain subsides, I tentatively roll my hips forward and back, watching his face contort with pleasure, as his hooded-eyes close and his nostrils flare.

"I'm giving this to you now, little girl," he murmurs, punching his hips upwards, almost dislodging me from his cock. "But don't become accustomed to taking control."

He pinches a nipple with his thumb and finger, a sharp streak of pain zipping through me like an electrical current.

"I would never…" I grin, asserting my innocence.

He opens one eye suspiciously. "And why should I trust you?"

Although said in jest, there's an underlying truth in his response. Trust and loyalty are hard to come by in our business. Deception is an aspect of our world and a necessity in the way we get our jobs done.

I couldn't even trust my own family, yet here I am, asking for him to have faith in me.

So, I say the only thing I can to ease his mind. This conversation is no longer about sex, really. It's about proving my reliability and integrity as a woman. And one that won't manipulate him to get what I want.

I rub my thumb over his bottom lip before bending down to kiss him, his lips parting as our tongues meet and merge.

When I pull back, I place his hand over my left breast.

"I give you my promise, just as I gave you my body. It's yours, Faron. I am yours."

CHAPTER 21

W e spent the rest of the night together, in between rounds of sleep and sex, Faron doing all sorts wicked and sexy things with my body. He introduced me to some light bondage, which he promised he'd play more with when we returned to the club.

I woke up this morning alone in the bed we shared, Faron in an adjoining room on the phone with presumably one of the brothers. I stretched and yawned, taking note of all the spots scattered around my body that I could still feel as a physical reminder of how he handled me last night.

My wrists had faint red abrasions from where he bound them together with a soft nylon rope tied to the headboard above my head as I kneeled, and he fucked me from behind. He whispered the most dirty and filthy things in my ears, suggesting how he couldn't wait to tie me up and tease my clit in front of an audience.

My face flushes even now as we walk down Saint Germaine-des-pres Boulevard toward the river, where Faron has reserved a tour boat to show me the historical beauty of Paris.

"What has you blushing so pink, little girl?" His arm secures around my waist, a finger digging into a ticklish rib.

I try to jump out of his grip, but he holds me firmly to his side.

"This is the first time I think I've ever felt happiness. My childhood was completely devoid of that emotion. But with you, I…"

"Belong." It's said without doubt or hesitation. "I understand that well, Gem."

We stand at the entrance of Pont Neuf, tourists of all national-ities and Parisiennes alike milling around past us, as Faron stops, turning to face me, and anchors my face in his palms.

"I can't promise you anything long-term, Gemma. I'm not structured that way and have far too many priorities competing for my attention. But I do know that since you've entered my life, you've captivated me in a way I'm still trying to comprehend. But know this…"

His dark eyes flicker with intensity, the warmth of his palms penetrating my skin and coloring my world with his presence.

"You. Belong. To. Me. And I don't want to let you go."

MY FEET and back ache from the miles of walking we did around Paris. Faron tried his best to give me a well-rounded tour in the short time we had available to us.

He took a picture with me at the Eiffel tower, and we saw the exterior of Notre Dame, the Arc de Triomphe, and the pyramids in the courtyard of the Louvre. I studied these places in high school, but never had the real-life experience to see them for myself.

My first-time in Paris was nothing short of perfect, punctuated by the fact that I got to spend it with the most handsome and beautiful man.

And now as we take the train back to Antwerp, I can't help but wonder if Faron will take me to the club tonight and fulfill his promises.

With my head on his shoulder and my hand wrapped around his arm, I lift my head to ask him what's on his mind.

"Will you take me to the Rough Edge tonight?"

My heart pounds in my chest, with anticipation and nerves over his response about taking me back to his private club, hidden inside The Edge nightclub veneers.

He snickers down at me. "Did all the things I said I wanted to do to you there pique your sexual curiosity?"

I nod briskly, eagerly. "Yes. But you mentioned something about sharing me."

There's a lump in my throat the size of a mountain, and I'm throwing this question at him without really knowing my own personal feelings about it. Did I want to be shared physically? Would I feel used and vulnerable? Or is the idea of being with other men while Faron watched or vice versa, appealing to my newfound kink awareness?

"I recall this...I would like that very much."

I worry my lips, hiding my face from his probing gaze. "Do you want to watch someone else...fuck me?"

"Absolutely not. Over my dead body."

"Then what do you mean by sharing me?"

Faron inhales a heavy breath and pinches the bridge of his nose. There's a moment of silence and then he sighs.

"It would make me happy to involve others in your sexual experiences. To give you pleasure using various sexual practices. And to do it in the presence of others."

And then my final question rattles him even more than the others. He goes visibly stiff next to me when I say, "Could we invite Roman and West?"

CHAPTER 22

We return to Antwerp that evening. Faron worked on the train and I napped after nearing exhaustion from the arduous day of walking the streets of Paris and only a few hours of sleep last night.

But the time we spent together today was romantic, and no matter what happens from here on out, it is something I'll cherish for the rest of my life. Although Faron hadn't shut down completely when I brought up interest in his brothers, there was a noticeable emotional distance that had been created by the time we stepped back inside Faron's home.

"I'm going to the office to make a few phone calls. Why don't you get ready for tonight? We'll have dinner out and then I'll take you to the club."

"Okay," I reply, climbing the stairs with an armful of shopping bags from the spree Faron took me on in Paris. "What time should I be ready?"

I stop midway up the stairway and glance back down to find Faron staring after me, his face indiscernible. I worry that

I've somehow made things uncomfortable between us. Me and my stupid mouth. I should have been fine with having Faron all to myself.

"I'll be back here by nine-thirty. And Gemma, I've made arrangements for your flight home. You leave tomorrow."

It hits me square in the chest, the words as sharp as an axe being thrown at a target.

I frown, my brows pinching together. "You what? You're sending me home so soon?"

He seems antsy for me to leave. "Yes, we've already discussed this. The sooner the better so we can finalize things and get what we came for."

Something in my brain shuts off. I can't seem to find the words to ask for further clarification. Didn't he just claim me as his? And now he can't get rid of me soon enough.

My heart drops to my toes. It feels battered and bruised, clinging to life support from a man who runs hot and cold and basically just gave me my walking papers.

I'm about to ask if he means he's coming with me or I'm going alone, but he's already left the room, heading to the garage door out the side of the house. Leaving me behind as if it's the easiest thing in the world to do.

Dumping out all the articles of lingerie and clothing he purchased me today, I sift through the pile, pulling off tags and choosing the perfect outfit for the club. Articles from La Perla and Agent Provocateur scatter across the bed in a rainbow of colors and styles.

As I step out of the shower, I try to decide if I want to dress to make Faron extremely jealous tonight or if I want him to beg for me to stay.

This time I don't have Serene to help me get ready, and I wonder if she has the day off or maybe she's on holiday. Either way, I curl my long auburn hair and let it cascade down my back in sexy, loose waves.

Better to grip and pull.

Oh God. All I can think about now is sex.

What is it about Faron and this new brand of kink and fetish lifestyle that resonates so deeply with me? Last night, he educated me on the various types of BDSM, fetish roles and sex toys used to stimulate and arouse during sex, providing both pain and pleasure. And then he even demonstrated on me, not only with the light bondage, but also clamps on both my nipples.

I touch my nipple through the silk of my robe, the sensation running straight to my clit that throbs in memory of his actions. Picking up the black lace and fishnet teddy, with its plunging V-neckline that opens to expose my cleavage and belly, with a built-in choker collar and G-string in the back, I pair it with fishnet stockings and lacy gloves with ribbon restraints, and I feel incredibly sexy. And naughty.

As I LOOK in the mirror, I plump my cleavage together with my arms pressed to my side. The strip of lace cascades from the collar barely covering my nipples, my tits firm and full. And then I bend over to check how it looks in the back.

There is nothing left to the imagination in this lingerie set, the G-string pulling tight in the crease of my butt. I can't wait for Faron's reaction when he sees me in it. And the slap of his hand against my backside that's sure to follow, leaving a nice red mark from his handprint. Or whatever instrument he decides to use.

Slipping on the long-sleeve, short, red sheath dress, it hugs my body like a glove, accentuating every round curve and my full breasts that are eager to be touched and sucked.

It feels like I've transformed into this new woman. Back home, I would hide my body, afraid of what people would say and what they would think when they saw me. But all I want to do now is flaunt what I have. Make Faron's mouth water and his cock hard when he sees me enter the room and make him so hot with lust that he'll bend me over his knee and swat my ass, telling me how his dirty slut has turned him into a horny beast.

I smile at my reflection and then practically jump out of my skin when his voice startles me out of my fantasy.

He stands close behind me, his hot breath at my ear.

"You are the very definition of cock tease in this dress, little girl. Every man that sees you will fantasize about being inside you," he observes, a hand trailing up the back of my leg and landing between my thighs where he strokes a finger over the new panties. "But they will only get to watch, touch and maybe even taste."

He slides the panel over my mound and glides a finger through my damp folds. I bite my lip, but the moan escapes anyway, my body yearning for everything he gives me. And then his finger breaches my entrance, plunging it inside my aching pussy.

"But I'm the only man, Gemma, who gets to be inside you. Do you understand?"

I nod emphatically and a sinful smile stretches across his face as he withdraws his finger, leaving me bereft.

"Good girl. Now come on, I've made arrangements that I think you'll agree with."

Sliding my hand through his crooked elbow, we head down the stairwell, where we stop in the foyer and he presents me with a box.

"Open it."

This is the first gift I've ever received from a man. The box is sealed with a bow, which I slide off and open the lid. Fishing around the tissue, my fingers land on a piece of leather. Faron takes the empty box from my hands as I lift the diamond-encrusted white neck collar, a small loop and lock in the front.

In our discussion last night, he mentioned the use of collars in the club worn by subs to represent they were taken and had a Dominant who they belonged to.

"I'd like you to wear this tonight."

I examine the soft fur lined interior of the leather accessory, my brain spinning with questions and confusion.

The collar represents a relationship of sorts. Boundaries and training, the forging of an ongoing union. Domination and ownership. But it's contradictory to the fact that he's sending me away tomorrow. Letting me go back to the U.S. without a definitive answer as to whether he wants me to return.

"Just tonight?" I question, my thumb skimming over the jewels in the ornate band.

His gaze flits away from me, his hands fisting at his sides. A tight tick in his jaw appears, visible even under the dark stubble of his five o'clock shadow, which never seems to disappear even after he's shaved.

Faron takes two steps closer, removing the collar from my hands and holding it between us before he lifts his eyes back to mine.

"I started slow with you, Gem, as inexperienced as you were. And it was good. You were so good. But I want to show you other ways...to do things to you..." He scrubs a shaky hand over his face and breathes a heavy sigh.

"This represents you are MINE in the club. You obey me and only me. You please ME. I choose what brings you pleasure and what pain to administer, no one else. This," he emphasizes, rattling the collar in his hand. "This gives me the responsibility and your permission to do that. And it will make me very, very happy."

I take the final step into him, turn around to kneel in front of him as I lift my hair from my neck, giving him my consent.

"Then I will gladly wear it, sir. I am yours."

CHAPTER 23

As it turns out, when we got to the club and Faron pulled Rome and West aside to tell them what I wanted to do with them tonight, West indicated that he was busy and excused himself to go take care of business.

But Rome, in all his sexy playfulness, jumped right on board.

"Well, it looks like my night just got much more interesting," he says with a flirty wink, wrapping an arm around my waist and pulling me in to place a kiss on the top of my head.

A growl springs from Faron's chest, as he unlocks Rome's hand from my hip. "Not until I say so. Go get a drink and meet us in the Amber room in twenty."

I lift a curious brow to Faron, who looks pissed off, as Rome steps away with his hands in the air. "Okay, whatever you want. Don't get your prissy panties all in a wad, jackhole."

Rome swats my ass as he flounces away, leaving me next to a surly Faron.

My fingers automatically reach for the collar around my neck. "Are you feeling okay about this?"

His terse response is opposite of the words he responds with. "Yes, why?"

I motion with my head toward the direction Rome heads off in. "Oh, I don't know. Maybe just the jealous tone I detected there with your brother."

He shakes his head. "He didn't have to be so handsy. He'll get his turn."

I stifle the giggle in my throat, reaching for his hand and lifting it to my collar. "This means I'm yours, sir. Just like you said. I'm open to whatever you want to do with me. Share me. Don't share me. Fuck me in private or in public. I just want to make you happy."

It's as if my words were the key to unlocking his mood, as his snarly frown turns into a soft smile and he pulls me in close with his finger in the ring in the collar.

"You make me crazy with desire and I suppose I'm letting that dampen our night together. I'm just not used to feeling this way about my…" He stops, dropping his hand and stares off into the crowd.

"Your what? Lovers? Submissives?" I press.

Our eyes connect and in it I see something I haven't seen before – fear. But I don't know what he could possibly be fearful of when it comes to me.

"Please, sir. Take care of me tonight."

He inhales several deep, measured breaths, lips tight in thoughtful concentration. And then his eyes narrow, growing pitch dark with need.

"Go wait for me on your hands and knees in the Amber room. Dress off and everything else remains on. You are to keep your eyes directed at the floor."

My stomach dips and flips, the excitement palpable and erotic energy unfolding in me as I get my first taste of his dominance tonight.

"Yes, sir," I respond dutifully and turn to make my way through the club doors and into my den of iniquity for the night, lust rolling through me with such force my knees nearly buckle.

Entering the room, the scent of amber is soft and faint, and I get my first glimpse of the room's atmosphere. Similar to what I saw the other night with Rome's threesome, there's a large bed with assorted hanging leather straps and shackles. Next to it is a table full of toys and instruments that seem to range from subtle pleasure to high intensity pain, as well as a swing of some sort hanging in the middle of the room, along with a spanking bench.

A shiver runs down my spine, tingles of anticipation, as I wonder what Faron might decide to use on me tonight. As he mentioned, he started off slow with me, and I know there's so much more he can do in the grand scheme of things to experience his sexual dominance.

There's a plush rug in the middle of the room where I drop to my knees, taking a look around me before I get the nerve to remove my dress.

It's liberating. Like shedding a layer of skin. Or stepping from my adolescence to adulthood.

I feel coolly confident in myself as I slip the dress off over my head and discard it on the bench next to the bed. While it's not cold in the room, goosebumps appear on my arms and legs, reminding me that I'm nearly naked, save for the tiny scraps of lace and silk covering my breasts and pussy.

Taking a fortifying breath, I bend forward and place my hands on the floor in front of me, my ass presented to the window behind me. The prospect of being watched by face-less voyeurs behind the frosted glass is titillating.

I don't know how much time has passed – it could be five minutes or thirty – but soon a door opens, and someone walks in behind me. Because my head is bent hanging between my shoulders, I can't see who it is. I want to ask, but I need permission to do so and I don't want to be disobedient.

My breathing accelerates as I hear him root around on the table, picking up one item at a time and returning it in its place until he seems to finally find something he likes.

He stands behind me so I still can't see his face, straddling me with one long leg on each side, and then his hand comes beneath my chin, lifting my head up with a quick jerk. With his other hand, he links a chain around the center loop of my collar, securing it with a click and then a tug.

I part my lips on a pant, my panties flooding with wetness even from just this innocuous action.

"Your safe word, little girl?" It's Faron's voice and it ignites every nerve in my body.

He'd discussed safe words the other night and the importance of having one ready in the event anything we did became too much for me to handle or bordered on a trigger. I assured him nothing he could do to me would push me too far, but he made me pick one.

"Diamond."

He gives a yank of the chain and then drops it to the floor. "Good girl."

Behind me he returns to the table, milling around for something until his deep voice commands that I comply.

"Get on the bed, spread eagle."

"Yes, sir."

I hop up on my feet and move to the bed, climbing on and immediately laying on my back, stretching my arms out in a V shape above my head, legs spread. I'm sure I look like a human X. Faron slowly comes around, first one side and then the other, restraining my wrists and ankles with the soft, leather cuffs that are attached to the bed posts.

"Twist your wrists to make sure they are secure but not too binding."

I do as he asks, feeling confident I won't lose circulation.

And then he picks up a black blindfold and steps up to the bed close to my face, pushing the satin material over my head and covering my eyes. Everything goes dark and I suck in my breath.

I listen hard to figure out what's going on when I hear the sound of the door opening and closing, and bare feet padding over the floor toward the bed. There's whispering, but I can't catch what's being said.

A few moments go by and then I'm startled when I feel the soft lick of leather being dragged over my exposed cleavage, down my belly until it rests over my pubic mound.

Snap.

The swish of the flogger is lightning fast and then there's a sting between my legs, and echo of my harsh rasp as it leaves my lips.

The rush of acute pain is followed by three more quick snaps and then someone's tongue sliding over my lace-covered pussy.

A groan of lust is followed by the sweeping motion of his tongue through my folds, the thong being pulled away to allow for full contact.

"I told you she was sweet, brother."

Faron's voice comes from in the front of my head, meaning it's Rome between my legs. I roll my hips experimentally but then a swat of the flogger at my breast stops me on contact.

"Don't move, little girl."

How in the world am I supposed to stay still when I have one Blake brother giving me pleasure with his tongue and another enjoying the view from above?

I moan and squirm, unable to comply with his command, for which I feel another painful snap across my nipple.

Rome swirls his tongue over my overly sensitive bundle of nerves, using his fingers to open my folds where his tongue lashes me more.

And just as I feel I'm about to reach that high pinnacle of satisfaction, Faron's mouth is on my breast, sliding the strip of fishnet out of his way and taking my nipple into his greedy mouth.

Words can't describe the intensity of the sensations that careen through me, every single cell in my body sparking as my legs quiver from the need to come.

"Faron...I'm so close. Please."

He bites my nipple between his teeth at the same time Rome sucks my clit between his, and I detonate. Just. Like. That.

As I slowly come down from my happy bliss, Faron unshackles my wrists and legs and repositions me on the bed, so my head is toward the bottom and now I'm on my hands and knees.

A pair of hands grip the edge of my panties and rips them down my legs, leaving me in only my garter belt and teddy.

"You're going to open and suck Rome, while I take this ass."

I swallow a worried lump in my throat. Faron runs a hand over the slope of my back, and then drizzles cold lube down my crease.

"I'll take care of you, little girl. Don't you worry."

CHAPTER 24

I t feels like my heart has been torn out of my chest, and I'm left empty and bleeding the moment my plane departed. I'd hoped against all hope that Faron would change his mind and come with me, especially after our time together last night. But instead, he sent Dempsey who occupies the seat next to me.

I shift in my seat, turning my face away from him, as my cheeks flush hot and my body responds to the memories of my experience last night. The way I was worshipped and watched and so thoroughly used by Rome and Faron. It was so perfect and everything I'd wanted it to be. I was there little girl, and they were my sun, moon and galaxy filled with stars.

West actually joined us last night towards the end, watching intently as Faron fucked me as I was suspended from the ceiling in a swing. At that point, I'd nearly blacked out from the four orgasms I'd already been bestowed, and the new sensation of having my ass taken for the first time.

Afterwards, I was so exhausted, I fell limply into Faron's arms and he brought me back to the Cove, showering me with aftercare and the sweetest words he'd ever said to me.

All my fears and doubts I'd had over my lack of sexual experience were quickly dismissed with every touch and caress from Faron. Becoming his submissive, and sharing the scene last night with the brothers, has done something for me. Has irrevocably changed me. Turned me into a woman no longer fearful of handing over control to a man, or worried of being hurt or abused.

With Faron, he's established boundaries and trust, and given me endless pleasure and praise.

But now, I miss it. I miss *him*. And an empty loneliness has settled in my heart, as breakable as glass.

When he dropped me off at the airport this morning, he didn't establish any timeframe for my return to Europe. It was left open-ended, supposedly to give me time to sort through my father's affairs, talk with Johno to get the information on the diamond's whereabouts, and figure out a plan if and when I do locate it.

All of it seems daunting and every minute of the flight I doubt myself and my abilities. Every additional mile of distance placed between me and Faron, I question whether what we shared together was real.

Is he just using you to get the diamond?

Do I mean anything to him?

I fall asleep sifting through the memories of last night, my goodbye this morning and the plans for when I land in Newark.

&

"MISS PHILLIPS? Wake up. We've landed."

Dempsey gently nudges my shoulder to rouse me from my sleep. I blink in confusion, rubbing my eyelids to adjust to the bright light of the morning sun streaming through the plane's tiny portal window.

"Thank you. Hope I didn't snore to loudly in your ear."

He chuckles good naturedly. "Only a little."

He stands and removes our carry-ons from the bins above, declining with a shake of his head when I try to retrieve mine from his hand.

We wait through the long U.S. Customs process which gives me time to put together my plan. I've decided to start with combing through the house to see if I can locate the original jewel. Mudd had his hiding places that I'd found by accident over the years as a kid, playing hide-and-seek games or trying to hide my candy or piggy bank money from my brother's greedy hands.

The Customs process this time around is less complicated then my experience in Antwerp, with nothing to declare and just my carry-on, so we head out to the taxi line to grab a car. As we wait in line, Dempsey texts Faron to let him we've arrived, and I get an odd sense that I'm being watched. The back of my neck tingles with the weight of someone's stare, which is ridiculous, I know, but I can't shake the feeling.

Twisting my head from side-to-side, I bend over, pretending I'm searching for something in my bag as I subtly look around as inconspicuously as possible. Noticing nothing or anyone out of the ordinary or equally nefarious, I shake off the strange vibe and step inside the taxi that's pulled up.

"Everything okay?" Dempsey inquires, slipping his phone back in pants pocket.

"Oh, yeah. How about with Faron? What did he have to say?"

Dempsey glances out the window, avoiding my eyes. "Nothing much. Just that I was to keep an eye out for anything out of the ordinary."

He whips his head back around. "So, if you see anything, you'll let me know."

I nod in agreement and give the driver my home address, as he takes off toward I-9 North toward Jersey City and Hoboken.

The weather is gray and dreary, a light mist of rain coating the filthy streets and highways. We pass brick and cement buildings a century old and over the Passaic and Hackensack Rivers cluttered with barges of containers, sewage seeping through the embankments littered with trash. Ah, to be home again. Although it's an ugly city and a world away from the beauty of Antwerp and Paris, I still feel the connection with my hometown.

The ride takes less than thirty minutes, as the taxi turns down Washington Street and parks along the tree-lined street. For all the shit Mudd put me through as a kid, he did a pretty good job picking out a decent neighborhood for me to grow up in. It's not the nicest part of town and certainly not the white picket fenced home of story books, but it's a quiet neighborhood with kids running around, a well-maintained park and a bodega on the corner.

Granted, there are drug dealers, pimps and gang members still winding through the streets, but they never bothered me and were just a fact of life growing up in this area.

I walk to the front gate, warped and turning a weird shade of green from the elements, and open it up, heading to the front door that has been barricaded with yellow police tape, warning violators of no entry. I swallow hard, as this makes my father's death all too real.

Until now, it was only words. Hearsay. But seeing this brings it all home. This is where my father was killed. And while he may no longer be inside, death has visited only recently.

Dempsey stops me with a gigantic arm across my chest, cross-guard style.

"Whoa, there. Hang on." His tone is a warning. He pushes in front of me, holding out his hand for me to relinquish the keys, which I drop in his palm for him to open it up.

I think Faron is being overly cautious for no reason. With my dad out of the picture, there's no purpose anyone would have to come looking for me. I can offer them nothing. I'm not the head of the family and don't have the network to run the business. I'm just a two-bit punk with a skill in thievery.

The same feeling I experienced while leaving the airport has returned, the hairs on the back of my neck standing on end with the sense that someone is watching me. Dempsey peels back the tape but struggles with the door, which always had a way of sticking and never seemed to get fixed. As he gives the key a turn and a nudge with his shoulder, I look behind my shoulder, scanning the cars lined up down the street.

.   .   .

THE DOOR CREAKS OPEN, the room shrouded in darkness, but the door gets stuck on something in its way. He pushes harder with an exhaustive grunt.

And then his alarmed voice cuts through the blaring street noises. "What the fuck is this?"

I try to peer around him but can't see past his big bulkiness, so I step onto my tiptoes, managing just enough leverage to see over his shoulder. And when I do, I gasp.

"Holy shit! My house...someone's ransacked it." I cover my mouth with my hand, staring wide-eyed at the disastrous mess that's been made in the living room.

Dempsey tries to block my entry, but I give him a hard shove to his side and barge through the entry. But I don't get very far when I find myself stalled in the middle of the room, turning side-to-side with all the contents strewn about like a tornado hit the house with a mighty force.

"Miss Gemma, I can't have you here. Mr. Blake would definitely not approve. It's not safe."

He backs me up with a gesture of his arm, withdrawing a gun from his pants that I hadn't noticed until now.

I try to rationalize with him, because I need to find that diamond. Or at least the trail that leads to the diamond.

"Listen, Demps. I know your job is to protect me, and I really appreciate that. But we don't know who was here or even when. The police could've tossed this place during the investigation. And if it was someone else, they're long gone. So, I'm sure we're fine. Plus, I have to find that diamond for Faron."

Dempsey gives me a wary look, considering the validity of my assertions. He keeps the gun in his hand but inclines his head in approval.

"Let me check around first. Stay put." He gestures toward the couch, which is missing several cushions, and I go take a seat.

As he meanders through the empty rooms, checking for intruders and marauders, I wring my hands together in worry, trying to decide where, if Mudd did hide it, could possibly be? Ticking off in my head all his old favorite hiding spots, where he'd hide wads of cash and contraband, I think of two possibilities. The floorboards under his dresser and behind the log pile in the back yard.

I jump to my feet, spinning around to run out the back door to check it out when I'm halted by the site of Dempsey being held at gunpoint, a gloved hand covering his mouth, blood spilling down his cheek from the gash in his temple, his wide eyes expressing dread and remorse.

"Oh my God!" I scream, ready to help, but the sound is muffled when a hand clamps down on my open mouth and my arms are pinned to my sides from someone behind me.

I thrash and kick to no avail, this guy's hold on me too strong to escape. From behind me I hear the dainty sound of *click-ety-clacks* against the wood floor, a pair of high heels echo to signal we have a new visitor in our midst.

Twisting my head with all my might, I drag my gaze to the finely dressed woman now standing in my entryway of my completely trashed house.

It takes me a moment for it to register in my foggy brain. She looks so familiar. How do I know her? Where have I seen her before?

My eyes squint and brows knit together as it finally dawns on me why I recognize her.

The expensive perfume and heels are the same as they were in Belgium. It's the same woman I met at the airport and who gave me a ride to the club.

"Hello, darling. Good to see you again, Gemma."

Dorian.

What the hell is she doing here?

CHAPTER 25

W hat the hell is going on right now?

Confusion wraps its long tentacles inside my brain like an octopus, and dizziness bleeds into corners of my vision as I fear I may actually pass out.

"Darling, you look so shocked to see me again. You're white as a ghost. Come, sit down."

Dorian gestures widely to the couch, giving the man holding me a signal to let me go. I'm honestly too stunned to try and escape, and I think she knows this. I flick a look at Dempsey, as she sees the direction of my gaze.

Her voice is steely venom. "Take care of him."

"Wait, what? No!" I yell, beseeching her not to do what I think she's going to do. "Please, let him go."

She pulls off a pair of fancy, Italian gloves, one finger at a time, and examines her manicure as if she's trying to decide whether to change her nail polish color. Completely disinterested in my protest to save Dempsey's life.

She *tsks* through a saccharine smile, her head cocked to the side in a patronizing tilt.

"Oh darling, aren't you just the sweetest," she sighs, leaning over to pat my hand with hers. I pull it back as if her touch is poison. Which it very might well be. "Let's consider a trade, shall we?"

My head is spinning so fast with a billion possibilities for the reason she's here. But I can't connect the dots.

A slew of questions tumbles from my mouth. "Who are you? What do you want? Why the hell are you here? Did you know who I was when we met?"

Under normal circumstances, her laugh would probably sound light and breezy, perhaps even friendly and warm. Instead, it's menacing and diabolical, a monster the likes of *Maleficent*.

Dorian crosses her legs, her black pencil skirt stretching tight around her thighs. She's dressed like a Manhattan socialite and her appearance in my home is marked with contradiction.

She places folded hands on her lap. "Let's see. Where shall I begin? Ah, how about with your father, Mudd. That bastard conned me and *stole* from me. Ironically, it was the diamond I paid him to steal for *me*, and then the double-crossing asshole offered to sell it to the Blake brothers."

My jaw drops open as I shake my head in disbelief. She knows Faron and his brothers? Oh shit, I need to warn him! I'm about to whip out my phone when I realize that I dropped my bags at the front door and my phone isn't with me.

It wouldn't matter anyway, considering I'm surrounded by bad men with guns and one swindled, pissed off woman who are watching my every move and will pounce with little provocation.

Which leads me to wonder if she had anything to do with my father's murder.

"Did you kill Mudd?"

Dorian feigns innocence with a hand over her heart. "Oh darling, it pains me to think you believe me capable of such heinous behavior."

I roll my eyes hard. "Cut the shit, Dorian. Enough with the righteous attitude. I know he was murdered by someone who he fucked over. And it stands to reason you fit the bill pretty well."

She lifts her delicate hands and steeples them under her chin, looking like a saint when in truth, she may be the worst sinner of all.

"It doesn't appear that I'm the only one, darling. Let's see, there's the Blake Brothers..." Her finger taps her chin before pointing toward me. "And speaking of fucked. I hear you've become very close to those three delicious men in a very biblical sense. You do realize that they only used you to get their rocks off. They'll discard you soon enough."

My face pales and a whoosh of white noise clouds my head. I blink rapidly, trying to tamp down my rage. I want to throw myself over her and gauge her eyes out.

"You bitch," I seethe. "Did you fucking have me followed? Were you watching me in Belgium?"

She lifts a bony shoulder with indifference. "I really did mean what I said when I dropped you off at their club that day. I warned you to turn around and go home. But you're either too stubborn or just young and dumb, and you fell for all that bullshit Faron throws on young women."

Her words are spiked with jealousy. Which can mean only one thing.

"Oh, you poor, sad woman. Now I get it. Faron fucked and dumped you, didn't he?"

Now I understand all the missing puzzle pieces and know what she wants.

The slap across my face is not expected and reminds me of all the backhands I received as a child from my father's quick, igniting temper. My head snaps back with the force of her hand, but I laugh at her reaction because now I have something to work with. Now I have a better understanding of who Dorian is and her motive.

Now I know what I have, and that she wants. Neither of which, however, I'm able to give to her. So, this whole situation is one that can't be easily resolved.

"Don't you dare speak to me like that, Gemma. And you best be prepared for the moment he turns cruel and callous, because believe me Gemma, that man loves no one except himself and his brothers. He will fuck you, mind, body and heart."

I almost feel sorry for her. Almost.

On one hand, one woman to another, I can empathize with pain of betrayal and the unreciprocated love from a man. I lived that every day of my childhood until I got to a point where I no longer cared.

And on the other hand, she needs to grow the fuck up. Even I know that sometimes love can hurt worse than the betrayal.

The sting of her slap rages red over my cheekbone, as I rub away the ache.

"Okay, Dorian. You warned me, I get it. But where does that leave us now? And for the record, I couldn't care less if you did kill Mudd. He may have been considered my father, but what he really was, was a monster. One that I wanted the hell away from."

Dorian leans over, jabbing her fingernail into chest above my heart.

"I want that diamond."

Join the club.

"I honestly don't know where it is, Dorian. And look at this place," I gesture around the room. "If you couldn't uncover it, how the hell do you think I will?"

"Because you'll have extra incentive."

I don't know what she means by this, until she twists around and flicks her gaze to the man holding the gun on Dempsey. She gives an infinitesimal nod of her chin.

There's a popping sound, like a cork being freed from a bottle, and then a grave *thump* as Dempsey lands in a heap on the floor. Blood drains from his head, pooling around the killer's feet, as he steps over it just as casually as he would a puddle of rain.

"Holy fuck," I gasp, my gaze floating between Dempsey and Dorian. And then back to Dempsey.

Oh my God, they just killed him. My stomach roils and threatens to spill its contents, which isn't much since we haven't eaten in hours. Swallowing hard, I turn back around toward Dorian, every muscle in my body tensing and ready to go to war.

"You crazy, fucking bitch."

She actually smiles at this. "It serves me well. Now, here's what we're going to do."

With a snap of her fingers, the big dude by the front door hands over my purse. She fishes around inside until she comes up with my phone. Handing it out to me, she says, "If you care about Faron and don't want the same fate to be his, you're going to call him and tell him that the deal he had with Mudd has been rescinded, and that you've decided to sell it to me. And then, you'll tell him it was fun, but it's over between you two."

There's a fissure of pain that slices through my heart. "No."

She gives me a patronizing look. "Ah, sweetie. You really do love him. Well, that's just sad, because I can guarantee you this. He won't put up a fight. He'll let you go faster than you can say the word diamond. Once he learns he can't get his product from you, there's no reason for him to keep you around."

"No," I repeat, the phone shaking violently in my hand. "I won't deceive him like that."

A gun to my head suggests otherwise.

"Oh honey, you can, and you will. And then you have 24 hours to get me that diamond. Now call the fucking man now before I really lose my temper."

My mind and body revolts with opposition as I pull up the number he'd programmed into my contacts before I left. With an arid mouth, I swallow, cringing at how I will possibly make this sound convincing. And praying that Dorian is dead wrong about the way he'll respond.

He answers on the second ring, and the sound of his voice nearly sends me to my knees.

"Hello, Gemma. Are you calling with good news, I hope?"

Pause.

Pause.

Pause.

"Gem? Everything okay, little girl?"

The use of nickname stabs me in the heart and makes me feel sick to my stomach for what I have to do.

"No. It's not good news."

CHAPTER 26

 fter the call ends, and the tears begin flowing down my cheeks, Dorian stands and wipes off her palms, a victorious grin covering her face.

"Darling, it was bound to happen. I'm saving you from the harsh reality of what would inevitably come later."

I hate her more than anyone I've ever hated in my life. Because Faron proved Dorian right.

He responded in the exact way she said he would.

He betrayed me. Manipulated me into thinking he cared about me, when in the end, he was only using me to get his fucking precious gem. I was simply a means to an end.

Even after I gave him everything. I think my love for him hurt worse than his betrayal.

Dorian interrupts my mini-pity party. "Clive here will stay with you, so don't get any hairbrained ideas about leaving. I'll pay you another visit tomorrow, shall we say seven p.m.?"

She glances down at her diamond-encrusted timepiece wrist-watch and flutters a hand in the air. "Okay then. Now, I'm off to the Met. I haven't seen an opera in ages. Ciao, darling."

Dorian actually has the gall to lean in and press a European-style kiss on both my cheeks. The very one she just slapped in anger and that is now damp from the tears that have fallen.

This woman is crazy insane. I honestly don't know how the hell I'm going to get myself out of this mess. I'm stuck between a rock and a hard place, and once again, I'm being held a prisoner against my will.

My only hope is to find this goddamn gem that's so precious to everyone involved, and with any luck, gain my freedom back.

Even if the price of my freedom is betrayal.

After she leaves, I remain on the couch, my head buried between my hands, my body racked with sobs, as the two men take care of Dempsey's dead body. I don't even bother trying to make a run for it while they are in dispose. Even if I could manage to escape, I have nowhere to go and no one left to turn to.

I'm alone in this world. The world I wanted so badly to escape and gain my freedom.

Laying my head down on the cushion, I tuck my feet under my butt and bring my knees to my chest and fall asleep.

I FIND the diamond in the second place I looked.

After falling asleep for a good three hours, a sound of a door opening and closing and the whispered grunts of Tweedle Dee and Tweedle Dumb wake me up. I lift my head, searching the room to find that Dempsey's dead body is now gone, and the blood stain has actually been removed.

Progress.

Using the bathroom to wash up, I'm praying the splash of cold water on my face might revive me enough so I can regain momentum and make some headway on locating the jewel. As I stare at my reflection in the mirror, I barely recognize myself with the messy bun and tear stains down my cheeks. Why do I look whole, when the heartache feels like a huge hole punched through my chest? I can't stand to remember what Faron said to me and the unnecessary cruelty he administered over the phone.

When I told him what Dorian forced me to say, he grew agitated and his breathing accelerated. While I couldn't see him, I knew his face was screwed tight, his jaw clenched, and his eyes narrowed in that menacing glare of his.

The problem, however, was that I couldn't tell what he was thinking. And his words…oh my god, his words slashed and obliterated everything we'd shared together like lacerations to my soul.

"No, it's not good news," I say, my heart pounding so loud I was sure it would wake the dead. "I believe you're familiar with a woman named Dorian."

There's a long silence and I can hear the cap of his pen clicking in the background.

Click, click, click.

"Yes, we're acquainted. What does she have to do with this?"

I want to scream at him for his choice of words. Acquainted made it sound like they met at a party in passing. Or at a gemstone conference in Switzerland. Not that he had carnal knowledge of her fucking pussy.

But I refrain from any of those remarks, because no matter what, I want to move on. And I want him safe.

My eyes flick to Dorian, who looks like she's about to come out of her skin with excitement, her face triumphant over my distress.

"Well, as it happens, my father had originally made the deal to sell her the diamond but reneged when he got your offer. And I believe in fulfilling promises, which means once I locate it, I'm selling it to her."

"Gemma, listen to me. You have no right to do that. We had an agreement. I thought we were in this together?"

I huff out a haughty response. "In this together? How can we be in it together if you walk away with everything and I am left with nothing?"

His voice descends a notch to barely a whisper. "Gemma, come on. Be reasonable."

I use this moment to twist the knife and see what he'll do. Will he fight for me or let me go?

"Faron, I think you've been using me this entire time. You held me against my will. Made me an accomplice for documents that didn't belong to you. And you've shared me with your brothers. Who the fuck does that? You don't care about me. I'm just an innocent girl in your precious, sick game.

We're done, Faron. Don't bother trying to contact me again."

When I hit end, my hand shook so hard the phone just fell to the floor, and I balled up onto the couch the minute Dorian left where I stayed until it grew dark.

I'd begun my search through the house, in the attic in my dad's closet, the boards behind the furnace, and the wall behind the stove, but everywhere turned up empty. I even searched the fridge, where I knew he'd hidden money from time to time, but that came up empty, too.

That's when I went out back, the Big Thug following closely behind, watching my every move.

"Hey, come on. At least make yourself useful," I say, removing chopped wood from the pile, and handing him them one by one. That's when I find it.

It was a hollowed-out log, like one of those electric fireplace log inserts, and I immediately knew I'd find it in there. I had to make a decision. With the Big Thug Clive standing right behind me I have to create a distraction and sleight of hand if I want to remove it from its present location. Or, I wait and retrieve it some other time.

The only problem is that the clock is ticking and if I have nothing to give Dorian tomorrow night, it could very well be the end for me. And I'll never get to make amends with Faron.

"Dammit," I grunt, picking up a huge armful of logs and setting them down next to the other discarded pile. "We need a shovel. I'm pretty sure it's buried underneath."

I glance over my shoulder to the shed, tilting my head as Clive follows my gaze. "Would you mind grabbing me one from in there?"

He eyes me suspiciously, rightfully so, but heads off to the shed, while I, in turn, quickly unearth the fake log and remove the jewel pouch. I slip it in my bra and adjust my shirt as Clive returns, shovel in hand.

We dig for over an hour, and of course we find nothing. Plopping down on my ass, I dust off all the dirt from my hands and my knees, acting disappointed and troubled.

"I thought for sure it would be here. I don't know where else to look."

It's getting late, well past ten by now, and although the jet lag isn't so bad returning to Jersey, I'm still hungry and tired. I push up to my feet and plant my hands on my hips.

"I think I'm done for now. I need to eat, shower and get some sleep. In that order."

He just shrugs his shoulders, neither concerned over or critical of my decision to stop for the night.

With nothing to eat in the house, and since I don't have a phone at my disposal, I ask Clive to place an order for a pizza while I go shower.

I strip down as the water warms up, carefully removing the diamond from my cleavage and holding the stone up to the light in my hand, examining its flawless beauty. The gem isn't as large as the Star of Africa, which I'd heard is the biggest diamond in the world, weighing over a pound before it was cut into smaller portions.

But this one is definitely beautiful, the light from overhead reflecting against its tiny grains, shining like a small disco ball, shooting its brilliant light across the room. Based on Faron's explanation of the gem, he had said it was roughly estimated at over 100-carats and could be worth anywhere from ten to twenty-million dollars.

Yeah, I get why all the cloak-and-dagger is necessary and maybe even why Mudd did what he did. That, I guess, I'll never know.

What I do know is that there is no way in hell I'm ever letting Dorian get her hands on this.

Some way, somehow, I'm going to make sure Faron gets what he was promised.

CHAPTER 27

After taking the longest, most needed shower in my life, I get dressed and hide the pouch between my legs, just like I'd done before first meeting Faron, before turning out my bedroom light and getting into bed.

I fall into a fitful sleep thinking of him and wondering when I'll ever get to see him again.

I'm woken with a start.

My lids burst open as a hand seals over my mouth. It's too dark to see anything and my eyes haven't adjusted yet, so my panic skyrockets as I squirm to get away.

But the voice is my savior.

Faron.

"How many are there in the house?" he whispers close to me ear, his hot breath soothing me from the panic that spiked through my veins when he woke me.

I hold up one finger and he nods. Removing his hand, he places his index finger to his lips and then a palm out for me to stay put.

I want to hug him and kiss him and drag him down on top of my body to thank him for coming to my rescue. I don't know how he knew I was in trouble, but he's here now and I'll find a way to make it up to him when I get a chance.

He points to the doorway, and then removes a pair of plastic ties, throwing them on the bed next to me. The same type he'd used on me originally in Antwerp. He mouths for me to wait and that when the time comes, he'd need my help.

I give him the thumbs up sign and slip out of bed to find my flannel shirt to cover myself. Faron quietly opens the door, holds his post for a moment before peering down the hallway. And then he's gone.

I think I hold my breath for an eternity as I wait for what's to come. I didn't notice a gun, but maybe it's hidden underneath the dark shirt he wears.

The silence is deafening, until I hear a weird gasp, and then thunderous groans and the bodily clamor and struggle of a man being choked to death.

I stay put, but worry claws at my very being, crippling me to the point where I begin to hyperventilate.

More scuffling, the sound of breaking glass, something heavy landing on the floor, a screech of pain and a loud curse. Banging thuds, one, two three. And then nothing.

I swallow, the sound loud to my ears, and tiptoe to the door to poke my head out, my voice coming out in a dry rasp. "Faron?"

I'm not even sure if the sound registers. I take a step out the door and try again a little louder this time.

"Faron?"

I lurch around the corner and flip the light switch on to find Faron laying on his side, holding his stomach with blood seeping out like a river flowing through his fingers.

Flying over to the floor, I land on my knees next to him. "Oh my god, baby. Are you okay?"

There is a large piece of glass sticking out of his belly, his sweater stained a bright red, his breathing labored and measured.

"Go find something to clean it up," he pants, pushing me away with his free arm.

My adrenaline kicks in now as I rush to the kitchen, grabbing the first bottle of alcohol I can find and several clean dish towels. Returning to the living room, Faron has scooched up against the back of the couch but is still slouched over and sweating profusely.

"You're going to have to help me." But his attention goes to Clive on the floor. I follow his gaze and see the guy twitching slightly. "First, tie his wrists together with the binders."

I do as he requests, fumbling as I loop them around his slippery hands, oily with blood. I watch for signs of consciousness, but he lays limp and nearly lifeless.

"Is he dead?" Faron asks, his head bobbing to the side, his eyes rolling back into his head.

I was never very good at playing doctor but I know the signs of a concussion.

"I don't know, and don't care. We need to get you taken care of. Is this your only injury?"

I poke and prod, looking for any other wounds or bleeding, but he's just bruised and sore around his knuckles and face. As I focus on the task of cleaning him up, I give him a swig of the vodka and get to work, rummaging in the bathroom for bandages and thread and needles, in the event I need to stitch.

Thankfully, in the end, the laceration proves not to be that deep as I remove his shirt to clean the wound, apply pressure and bandage him up around his belly and waist.

Satisfied that things are stable, I help him up onto the couch, careful to avoid jostling him too much, and I sit down next to him.

"Did you really feel I used you? That I don't care about you?"

My heart plummets to my feet, the guilt of having said those lies burning like acid in my stomach.

I take his hand, bringing it to my lips and kissing his knuckles one by one.

"No, it was all lies. I'm sorry. She made me say all that. She harbored some pretty deep-seated resentment toward you, and this was her way of getting back at you."

He groans, clutching at his side as he shifts on his hip to face me.

"I knew you didn't mean any of it, Gem. You sent a distress signal and I heard it through every word you spoke. That's why I hopped the first flight out. I knew you were in trouble.

It was also pretty clear when I didn't hear back from Dempsey."

Oh God, how could I have forgotten?

"I'm so sorry, Faron. They killed him. I watched as they shot Dempsey and then disposed of his body. She said if I didn't want the same thing to happen to you, I'd do as she demanded."

Faron strokes my face gently, tucking my wild hair behind my ear and kissing the side of my cheek.

"There was nothing you could have done. I'm just glad you're okay and they didn't hurt you."

"What do we do about Dorian now? She's planning on returning tomorrow night."

He laces his fingers through mine, settling back against the couch and closing his eyes, wincing with every breath he takes.

"We'll be long gone by then. Plus, there's nothing here for her to claim. You didn't find the diamond."

Tugging my hand free from his, I slip it inside my shorts, the move gaining Faron's attention as he cracks a lid open to see what I'm doing.

Giggling when he arches a sexy brow, I reach down and nab the pouch out of my panties, wiggling my hips in a slow, sexy maneuver. When I pull it out, I slide the loop through my finger and dangle it in from of him, an enticing offering just for him.

"I think you may have been looking for something like this," I say in a seductive tone, swinging it in front of him. "So, what's it worth to you?"

He chuckles and tries snatching it away, his reaction time delayed and slow due to his injury and I hold it just out of his reach.

Faron slowly moves to his knees, his hand still pressed into his abdomen, hovering and moving over me, and crushes his mouth to mine. I part my mouth and moan as he slides his tongue inside, savoring my taste and exploring every inch of my mouth.

When he pulls back, I'm panting and restless.

"There's no diamond in this world as precious or as priceless to me as the Gem I'm staring at right now."

My heart floods with happiness, as I wrap my arms around his neck and nuzzle into his intoxicating scent.

"I'll give you everything and more if you say you love me."

I smile into his neck. "I love you, I love you, I love you."

THE END

EPILOGUE

6 months later - Roman

I FIDGET WITH MY TEN-THOUSAND-DOLLAR, diamond-encrusted watch, a gift from the groom, as I wait impatiently for my brothers, West and Faron, to arrive.

I've been waiting in the anterior room of the old Gothic cathedral in the heart of Paris now for over fifteen minutes, while the groom and groomsmen got ready down the hall.

I chose to wait, already having come dressed for the occasion, in a room so dark and medieval, the stone walls practically screaming of stories untold of dungeons and knights locked deep within its confine; filled with centuries of weddings, baptisms, and funerals that have occurred inside these cathedral walls.

All related to death in my opinion.

My tuxedo and cummerbund feel abnormally stifling, much like the cloistering effects of the small room, even though I frequently wear this suit to black-tie affairs. But today it chokes my breath and my throat constricts every time I try to swallow.

You'd assume the panic clawing up my spine is the stress related to my own wedding day. A day that equates to the loss of freedom and a future filled with only one woman for the rest of your life. The day you're shackled with the proverbial ball-and-chain.

But no, it's not my sentencing day. It belongs to my older brother Faron, who is marrying his fiancée, Gemma. The woman he met under the strangest of circumstances and who we ended up holding for ransom in order to get the jewel we'd been promised by her father.

Ironically, in a strange turn of events, her father double-crossed us, and then ended up being murdered. Not by our hands, although if we'd had it our way, my brothers and I would've done the deed ourselves. Because that's what you do to protect someone you love. And Faron truly loves his Gem.

I suppose my actions could be construed as similar based on what I did to protect Serene the night her life was in jeopardy. The night a very powerful man thought he could have her without her permission.

Without *my* permission.

That's the kicker in this bizarre and twisted tale. Until that night, I hadn't even realized that I was in love with Serene. I didn't grasp just how deep my attraction for her really went and how far I would go to save and protect her.

With her gorgeous brown skin, luminous silver eyes, and a body that made any man in her vicinity beg to have her, there's no question I wanted her the minute I laid eyes on her.

But I didn't beg. I made *her* beg.

Which she did on her own volition many times over the past year. She begged for me while on her knees before I would fuck her mouth with my cock. Or while on her back with her legs spread wide, each ankle tied to the posts on the bed, her luscious cunt dripping with arousal as she cried out for me to take her hard.

And holy fuck, she was the best I've ever had. No one else since has even come marginally close to what Serene did to me. She is an ever-constant reminder of what I can't have and it's for her own good that things happened the way they did.

I reassured myself it wasn't love. Love was only an illusion and didn't exist in my world. It was simply a dark, haunting lust. A deep, passionate, spine-thrilling lust that kept her in my thoughts every waking moment of the day. And every long, sleep-deprived night without her.

Then one night the unthinkable happened and I did the only thing I could to protect her. To save her from the world I'd created for her. The world where my actions and the people I associated with finally unveiled what a monster I'd turned into.

And to redeem myself, I had to remedy the problem.

What I did to save her was the right thing - even though it caused irreparable harm and severed our connection.

Even after moving her out of the club for her own good and into a secure location as Faron's assistant, providing her a protected workplace, she hates me for it. She no longer looks me in the eyes. And when and if she does, her silvery-luminescent gaze is filled with fiery disgust and hatred toward me.

Can I blame her?

What I did had to happen to save her from further harm. To save her life and keep her from being taken from me. Things had to be done to ensure my precious beauty would always be near.

"Hey, you got the rings I gave you?" Faron interrupts my self-loathing thoughts as he steps into the room, wearing a similar tux and a blue flower on his lapel. Weston files in behind him, looking uninterested and bored – his normal expression.

I pat my front pocket and nod. "Of course. I wouldn't let anything happen to these precious gems."

Faron, my older brother, looks pleased with my efforts and squeezes my shoulder. "Thanks. And how about the flask?"

Chuckling, I waggle my brows and extract the small sterling silver flask from the inside of my jacket, unscrewing the top and handing it to him.

As he takes a healthy swig, I make sure to get my jabs in now before the processional begins. "You know you still have time to back out if you're that nervous. Or sign the prenup."

This was a sticking point between me and Faron in the weeks leading up to this day. I was opposed to the fact that he didn't require a prenuptial contract between him and Gemma. It made no sense to me knowing we'd built this empire as a family and now Gem could easily take it away from all of us with just the click of a pen.

It's not that I don't like Gem or trust her, but she's an outsider. An American jewel thief who didn't have a dime to her name before she met us. She lived under her criminal father's thumb, and they'd already shown us the lengths they'd go to in order to get what they wanted. Although her father is no longer with us, the wounds are still fresh, and for me they haven't yet healed over completely for me to feel one hundred percent comfortable with Gem. But we're getting there.

However, Faron wouldn't listen to my concerns. He's given his heart to Gemma and trusts her implicitly. He has found the woman who he loves enough to marry, and therefore says he will honor her with his trust. And his fortunes.

Faron stares me down with a mutinous glare. "Enough with that shit, Rome. We've gone over this, and it's done. Today is about love and celebration."

"And lots of fucking," chimes in West, who lifts his head from his phone with a smirk.

We all laugh at the truth in West's statement. In fact, I'm pretty sure Faron has already indulged in some pre-marital fornication earlier this morning with his bride-to-be, the insatiable fucker. The look of satisfaction is written all across his face.

Faron has certain appetites and proclivities that his once virginal fiancée has become very fond of. Before they were engaged, I even got in on some of the fun, because that's how we roll in our family. West, on the other hand, is a bit more reserved with his preferences. And that's okay. More for me.

But lately, Faron and Gem have kept their sex life a bit more private, away from the exposure our club offers lovers who enjoy the thrill of sexual exhibition.

A knock on the door sounds the warning that the ceremony is about to begin. "It's time," says the clergy assistant as he peaks in the crack through the door.

Faron heaves in a deep breath and returns to the flask to me. I take a large gulp and offer it to West, who casually shakes his head. Recapping the lid, I slide it back into my inside jacket pocket and smack Faron on the back.

"Well, although you didn't heed my warnings, I still love you, brother, and I'm behind you one hundred percent. Now let's go get you hitched."

West opens the door and walks out in front, followed by Faron and then me. We head down the long, marbled hallway to a small arched doorway leading into the chapel where the priest is already in waiting.

The pews are filled with hundreds of friends and business acquaintances, mostly those we know, as Gem has no family or friends here in Europe or Paris, specifically.

However, she has grown friendly with Serene. In fact, Serene is her only bridesmaid and maid of honor today. My entire body tightens at the knowledge that I'll be sharing the evening with the elegant beauty tonight, which I hope might lead to a rekindling of sorts later.

Maybe if I'm lucky, I'll find a way to get her alone, push her up against a wall in one of these low-lit alcoves, slip my hand underneath her silky dress and bury my cock deep inside her.

One can always hope.

The music of the processional begins, filling the rafters with the sounds of a pipe organ and drowns out my internal porn reel, as the double doors open for the wedding party to enter the sanctuary.

Closing my eyes against the flood of emotion, I steel myself against what I know will have a profound effect on me, as I watch Serene walk down the aisle toward the pulpit. Breathing in my resolve, I open again, and in a flash I'm assaulted by her elegant beauty. Like a goddess or princess. An ethereal angel.

Her lavender silk gown drapes over her lush curves, exposing her dark, flawless smooth skin. Her hair is done up in a fancy chignon, a sparkling barrette clasped on the right side. Her cheeks glow with a pinky color, her silver eyes outshining even the brilliance of the diamond necklace that falls between her breasts.

And then she lifts her eyes and finds mine, latching on as if we're tethered together as she walks forward in her graceful strides. My breath falters, as if lightning has struck my heart with a flash of the future and steals every doubt that has been buried within me.

A future where I'm not the best man and she's not a bridesmaid.

A future in which she doesn't despise me for ruining her life.

A future where it's just the two of us together in this moment, where we're not the ones standing up at someone else's wedding.

ACKNOWLEDGMENTS

To Arti Nihalani – my Bollywood dancing, Zumba queen and Precious Treasures jewelry store owner extraordinaire friend. Your schedule was crazy and packed with travel all over the world, but I appreciate you taking the time to share your insights with me on the jewelry and gemstone wholesale business. It was fascinating to learn about the process, and even though I only used a small portion of the research notes, it fueled my imagination to help craft this story. Thank you!

To Julie Kuykendall and Bryan Burgmaier for connecting me with a local jeweler. Thanks for your continued support of my writing endeavors, my friends!

To Christine Yates, my proofreader with Piece by Piece. Your advice and suggestions are always appreciated. Love you, girl.

Lastly, to my readers. This book was a new venture for me. A little darker, a bit suspenseful and definitely different from my normal writing style. I hope you enjoyed it and I appreciate you giving it a read. Sometimes we have to step out of your normal routine and try something new – which is exactly what I did with the *Precious Gems* story. It challenged me to think in a different way and to write outside my comfort zone.

I hope your interest is piqued and you'll want to learn more about Roman and Serene in the upcoming book, *Precious Beauty* (The Blake Brothers #2).

ABOUT THE AUTHOR

Sierra writes new adult and sizzling hot contemporary romance. She's written and published 24 novels, including the award-winning college sports series, *Courting Love* and the twice award-finalist erotic ménage serial, *Reckless – The Smoky Mountain Trio*.

Her latest new adult/college romance series, **Change of Hearts** is available NOW only on Amazon Kindle Unlimited.

Sierra lives with her husband and dog in the Seattle area. She is a sucker for cheap accessories, loves anything dark chocolate, and enjoys rocking out at live concerts.

Subscribe to her email list here: www.sierrahillbooks.com

ALSO BY SIERRA HILL

Change of Hearts (A Standalone College Campus Series)

Game Changer (Single Dad/Nanny)

Change in Strategy (An Office Romance)

Courting Love (A College Sports Series)

Full Court Press

The Rebound

Pivot

Fast Break

Jump Shot

Reckless – The Smoky Mountain Trio

(Menage serial)

Reckless Youth

Reckless Abandon

Reckless Hearts

Reckless – The Smoky Mountain trio boxset

The Physical Series (An Erotic series)

Physical Touch

More Than Physical

Physical Distraction

Physical Connection

Standalones/Flirt Club